PAGAN ENCHANTMENT

Merry Charles was a promising young actress and Gideon Steele a very celebrated director—and when he came to see her play one night she couldn't help hoping it meant he was going to offer her a job in his next production. But that wasn't what Gideon wanted at all!

Books you will enjoy
by CAROLE MORTIMER

HEAVEN HERE ON EARTH

Mark Montgomery was a good friend of Ryan's—nothing more—and it was in a friendly spirit that he had offered her the use of a cottage on his family estate in Yorkshire for a holiday. But his overbearing older brother Grant chose to misunderstand the whole situation, and the holiday turned into a very exhausting battle of wills. Could Ryan possibly win it?

LOVE UNSPOKEN

'You're so busy trying to do your job as well as a man you've forgotten how to be a woman!' Zach Reedman had thrown bitterly at Julie—and so they had parted for good. Yet, three years later, Zach had turned up again, announcing that he was going to marry the sweet, gentle Teresa Barr. Was it really the end of everything between them now?

FANTASY GIRL

One of the reasons Natalie's modelling agency was so successful was her biggest customer, Thornton Cosmetics—but now its formidable head, Adam Thornton, was threatening to close his account unless her top model Judith mended her ways! But how could Natalie do anything to harm Judith?

UNDYING LOVE

From the moment they met, Rick Dalmont had made it plain that he wanted Shanna. But Rick had 'wanted' plenty of other women in his time—and tipped them on to the rubbish heap the moment the novelty had worn off. Why should Shanna add herself to their number?

PAGAN ENCHANTMENT

BY
CAROLE MORTIMER

MILLS & BOON LIMITED
15–16 BROOK'S MEWS
LONDON W1A 1DR

All the characters in this book have no existence outside the imagination of the Author, and have no relation whatsoever to anyone bearing the same name or names. They are not even distantly inspired by any individual known or unknown to the Author, and all the incidents are pure invention.

The text of this publication or any part thereof may not be reproduced or transmitted in any form or by any means, electronic or mechanical, including photocopying, recording, storage in an information retrieval system, or otherwise, without the written permission of the publisher.

This book is sold subject to the condition that it shall not, by way of trade or otherwise, be lent, resold, hired out or otherwise circulated without the prior consent of the publisher in any form of binding or cover other than that in which it is published and without a similar condition including this condition being imposed on the subsequent purchaser.

First published 1983
Australian copyright 1983
Philippine copyright 1983
This edition 1983

© Carole Mortimer 1983

ISBN 0 263 74353 5

Set in Monophoto Times 10 on 11 pt.
01-1083 – 53015

Made and printed in Great Britain by
Richard Clay (The Chaucer Press) Ltd,
Bungay, Suffolk

For
John and Matthew

CHAPTER ONE

'DID you see who was in the audience?' Vanda asked excitedly at the end of the first act, as the two of them were changing for their next scene.

'Who?' Merry asked wearily, knowing there was always supposed to be 'someone' in the audience. There rarely was, and somehow she doubted it very much for this play—it would probably be closed down within the week! A dozen or so inexperienced actors and actresses parading about the stage wearing weird clothes and having shocking coloured hair—her own was pink!—spouting inane dialogue to the meagre audience, was not something that was likely to attract the interest of anyone who really mattered. In fact, it no longer held her interest—and she was appearing in it!

'Gideon Steele!' Vanda pulled on her own tight leather trousers and leather waistcoat, her hair bright orange, her own blonde hair hidden beneath the atrocious wig.

'Don't be silly,' Merry dismissed, putting on a similar outfit, hating the amount of bare flesh it left. This play might have paid her rent for the last month of rehearsal, but even though it would once more leave her one of the numerous unemployed, she would be glad when it came to an end. It would probably never have opened at all if Harry Anderson, the author, hadn't been rich enough to pay to have it put on himself. All it had proved was that you could put anything on the stage if you had the money to pay for it. Nevertheless, the critics would close this play as soon as possible;

even Harry Anderson couldn't expect them to play to an empty theatre! Although having come to know Harry this last month she thought maybe that wasn't so unbelievable. Left a millionaire many times over three years ago when only twenty-two, he had more money than sense, as her father would have put it.

As for Gideon Steele being in the audience, it was not only unlikely, it was highly ridiculous. He had won an Oscar last year for best film director, his work being highly acclaimed by fellow directors and critics alike. And he wouldn't come to see a play like this. Besides, he was a film director, not a stage director.

'Handsome Harry said he is,' Vandà used their pet name for Harry Anderson.

'Wishful thinking,' Merry grimaced. 'Come on, the second act is about to start. And in case you forgot, we should be on stage.'

'Okay,' the other girl shrugged. 'But take a look in the front row. I only saw him on the box last year at the awards, but I don't normally forget a good-looking man,' she gave an exaggerated leer, 'and Gideon Steele is a handsome devil. In fact, he's gorgeous! I'm sure it's him. Your mascara has run.' Vanda handed her a tissue. 'God, this make-up is awful!' She shook her head.

It certainly was. Stage make-up was always thick, necessarily so because of the lights, but as they played the parts of two showgirls their eye make-up was very thick too, their lip-gloss a deep slash of red across the mouth.

The second act went as badly as the first, and Merry saw several people actually get up and leave. But not the man sitting alone in the very front row, several vacant seats away from other people. She couldn't see him clearly, just caught glimpses of him every now and then, a dark-haired man wearing glasses with tinted lenses, making it impossible for her to see the colour or expression of his eyes. He was sitting back in his seat, the ankle of one leg resting on the knee of the other one, the elbow of one arm resting on the side of the chair, his hand up over his mouth partly obscuring his face.

'Did you see him?' Vanda asked as they came off to prepare for the third and final—perhaps in more ways than one!—act.

'I saw *a* man,' Merry nodded. 'But the way he's hiding his face he could be anyone.'

Vanda giggled. 'You'd probably hide your face too if you were Gideon Steele watching a play like this!'

'*If* he is Gideon Steele.'

'He is,' Harry spoke from behind them.

Vanda spun round. 'He is?' her pretty face lit up, although she looked very garish in the bright make-up. 'He really is?' She grabbed Harry's arm.

'Yes, darling, he really is,' he drawled, his fair hair brushed back from a middle parting, a white silk scarf draped casually around his neck, falling loosely down over the black evening jacket he wore. His features were almost too perfect, making him occasionally look beautiful, like right now, aptly earning him the nickname of Handsome Harry. 'But he isn't here to see you,' he told Vanda smugly. 'He's here to see Merry.'

Her head went up. 'Me?' she gasped. 'You really mean me?'

'Well, he took me to one side and asked me to point out which one was Meredith Charles. He said you all looked alike,' he added with a disgusted sniff.

Merry frowned. 'But why would he want to see me?' she puzzled.

'Use your head, darling,' said Harry in his most affected drawl. 'He's casting his latest movie, maybe there's a part in it for you.'

'Step on to my casting couch!' Vanda giggled. 'I might even be persuaded to do that for a man like him.'

'Really, darling,' Harry drawled haughtily, 'do have some class! That approach is old hat now. And you, darling,' he spoke to Merry, 'make a good impression, there's a love.'

'"There's a love",' Vanda mimicked softly as he moved away. 'Do you know why he calls us all darling or love?'

'Why?' Merry asked vaguely, wondering if Gideon Steele really did have her in mind for his next film. What a break that would be if he did. This awful play would have been worth it!

Vanda grimaced. 'Because he can't remember our names.'

'Who can't?' she frowned.

'Handsome Harry can't. Hey, are you with me?' her friend teased.

'Sorry,' she smiled. 'I was just—I can't believe Gideon Steele asked to see me!'

'Fantastic, isn't it?' said Vanda without jealousy, her arm through the crook of Merry's as they went to the dressing-room they shared with two other girls.

Merry was very nervous when she went back on stage, even more conscious of the man sitting alone in the front row. His hand was down from his face now, revealing deeply tanned skin, a long straight nose, the well-shaped mouth twisted derisively, the tinted glasses still hiding his eyes. Merry had always believed the eyes to be the mirrors of the soul, and without seeing his eyes she couldn't begin to tell what he was thinking. But that derision on his mouth made her squirm.

By this time the theatre was slowly emptying, so that by the time they came to the end of the play the clapping in the darkened theatre sounded to be half a dozen people. And Gideon Steele wasn't one of them, getting to his feet and going through the stage door to the right of him. Merry had a brief glimpse of him before the curtain came down, a tall powerfully built man, wearing fitted denims and a brown bomber jacket.

'Wonderful, darlings. Wonderful!' Harry enthused ecstatically as they wandered off the stage.

'It may have escaped your notice, Harry,' one of the male cast taunted, 'but the damn theatre was empty by the time we got to the end!'

'Exactly!' he cried. 'That's exactly the reaction I was looking for.'

'Idiot!' hissed Vanda.

'I don't know what you're all complaining about,' he snapped. 'You have nothing to lose——'

'Except their reputations as actors,' drawled a sardonic voice.

'Gideon!' Harry exclaimed with a smile. 'My dear man! What did you think of it?'

Merry was busy studying the man she now knew was Gideon Steele. He stood only feet away from her, taller than any of the other men here, older too, with an aura of power and vitality that seemed to make him impatient with his surroundings. His hair was very dark, almost black, brushed casually back from his face and long over his collar and ears, the face hard, as if carved from granite, the glasses still in evidence and so shielding the expression of his eyes.

He looked at Harry unsmilingly. 'It was trash,' he said bluntly. 'And that's being kind.'

Harry's mouth dropped open, a hurt look to his face. 'Gideon...'

'And who gave you permission to call me your dear man, boy?' he snapped, using his obvious seniority to humiliate the other man. 'You ought to be put against a wall and shot for the setback you've given the reputation of the theatre tonight. In fact, I'd like to be the one to do the shooting,' he derided harshly.

Several of the cast members turned away to hide their smiles, but not Merry. She knew the play was awful, that they must all have been mad to appear in it, that without his own money to back it Harry would never have got it as far as a theatre, but that didn't excuse the way Gideon Steele was verbally humiliating the other man in front of everyone. It was cruel and unkind—but then Gideon Steele had a hardness about his mouth that seemed to indicate he enjoyed being cruel on occasion.

'I'm sure we all have our failures when we first start out,' she heard herself say. 'Even you, Mr Steele,' she added softly, holding her breath at her own daring.

She had remembered something about Gideon Steele, something she had read about him once. He may be a highly acclaimed director now, but when he had started out fifteen years ago he had had an absolute disaster of a film, had had trouble getting finance for future films, and it had taken the succeeding five years to prove his skill. But he had been at the top of his profession for ten years now.

He looked over in her direction, everyone about them suddenly falling silent, the ones that had been rushing off to change now lingering on at the prospect of a heated exchange. 'Touché, Miss . . .?'

'Charles,' she supplied stiltedly.

His mouth tightened. '*Meredith* Charles?'

'Yes.'

He turned furiously to Harry. 'You told me the one with the orange hair!' he ground out.

Harry looked uncomfortable. 'I'm sure I said pink . . . Does it matter?' he shrugged dismissively.

The other man controlled his anger with effort. 'Not now,' he sighed. 'I'd like to talk to you, Miss Charles,' he told her impatiently.

The buzz of interest deepened about them, and Merry felt herself blush. Whatever he had to say surely shouldn't be said in front of the rest of the cast?

Obviously he thought so too, for he took her arm in a firm grip to move her to one side of the corridor, out of earshot of the others, most of them starting to wander off to their dressing-rooms now, losing interest when it was obvious he had come to see Merry and not themselves.

'Do you mind?' She shook off his hand, conscious of the speculative looks she was receiving; some of her fellow actors obviously doubted that this man's interests were professional—as she did herself. He hadn't even realised which one she was, had thought Vanda was her!

Someone pushed by them, momentarily knocking Gideon Steele off balance, so that for a moment Merry was crushed between the wall and the hardness of his body. She wasn't very tall herself, only five feet two, and consequently her face was squashed against his chest, his thighs grinding into her.

'Hell!' he muttered, moving back. 'It's impossible to talk here. Go and change, I'll wait for you outside.' He pushed the tinted glasses up the bridge of his arrogant nose. 'Don't be long.'

'Mr Steele!' Her angry outburst stopped him in the process of turning to leave.

His brows rose. 'Yes?'

She frowned her consternation. 'I'm sure you're a brilliant director, in fact, I know you are——'

'You surprise me,' he drawled, 'after appearing in this garbage.'

Her eyes sparkled angrily. 'I have to pay the rent, Mr Steele. And if appearing in this "garbage" can do that, then I'll do it!'

His mouth twisted, his eyes just discernible now, although not the colour. 'You had to be desperate.'

Merry's mouth tightened at his insulting tone. 'I'm not so desperate that I'll meekly agree to meet you when I've changed! I've heard of Gideon Steele, of course, and Harry seems convinced you are who you say you are, but I think we're all agreed that Harry is an idiot.'

'And after you defended him so bravely a few minutes ago,' he taunted.

'You were ridiculing him!'

'He deserves to be ridiculed! If I had my way he would never be allowed near a theatre again,' Gideon Steele bit out angrily.

Merry gave a half-smile. 'He probably never will be.'

'No,' he agreed ruefully. 'So if you don't think I'm Gideon Steele, just who am I?' he mocked.

She shrugged. 'I have no idea.'

'But you don't intend meeting me later to find out?'

She looked at him unflinchingly. 'No.'

'So I need someone—other than Harry Anderson,' he derided, 'to vouch for me?'

'There's no need to go that far,' she snapped. 'Perhaps I could meet you somewhere tomorrow?'

He gave an impatient sigh. 'Would you feel safer with me in daylight?'

'I would feel *safer* if I never saw you again,' she told him coldly, her head at a haughty angle. 'But if you really are Gideon Steele . . .?'

'Yes?'

'I would be a fool not to at least listen to what you have to say.'

'More so than you realise,' he nodded grimly.

'Okay, we'll meet tomorrow. Do you have anywhere in mind?'

His derision rankled. After all, she hadn't been born yesterday, and she had heard too many stories from friends of hers that had warned her to beware of the men who promised sudden fame. Even in this day and age it wasn't unheard-of to be fooled by these men. She would be stupid to go off into the night with a man she didn't even know.

'The Ritz, I think,' she told him airily. 'For lunch.'

His mouth twitched. 'One o'clock?'

To his credit he hadn't even flinched at her choice of one of London's leading hotels and restaurants. Perhaps he was Gideon Steele after all; his arrogance certainly seemed to say he was.

'One o'clock will be fine,' she nodded, deciding she had pushed her luck far enough for one day—or night. Goodness, she was tired, and if she didn't soon get this heavy make-up off she would break out in a rash. 'If you'll excuse me . . .'

'Meredith——' his hand grasped her arm, the skin firm and tanned, with a light sprinkling of dark hair, the fingers long and tapered, very strong, as he held her immobile.

She looked from that hand into the hard, inflexible face. 'Yes?' She suddenly felt breathless.

'Don't let me down,' he instructed softly. 'It's too important. All right?'

'All—right,' she nodded, wishing the tightness away from her chest. And miraculously it was as he released her. 'Good—goodnight.' She went into her dressing-room, not looking back, although she wanted to, if only to see if he were still there.

'Well?' Vanda pounced on her excitedly as she entered the room, looking more like her normal self, her short blonde hair now in evidence, the thick make-up removed now, showing her own clear complexion and sparkling blue eyes.

'Well what?' Merry said absently.

'Has he offered you a part in his next film?'

'Not yet.'

Vanda frowned. 'What does that mean?'

She shrugged. 'I don't know. It's eleven-thirty at night, much too late to be discussing anything. I'm exhausted! We've arranged to meet tomorrow,' she revealed reluctantly, knowing Vanda wouldn't rest until she knew everything. 'For lunch,' she supplied before the other girl asked, and pulled the pink wig off with a sigh of relief, taking the pins from her ebony-coloured hair, allowing it to cascade in gleaming waves down her back, the feathered fringe swept back either side of her small heart-shaped face. Next came the make-up, and her skin really started to feel uncomfortable. 'Ugh!' She removed the artificial lashes, cleansing her eyes of the black clog applied to them earlier, instantly looking more like her twenty years without the cheap image she had projected on stage.

'Sounds promising.' Vanda sat cross-legged on the sofa that was pushed against one wall of the small room. The two girls were the only ones left, the others having already gone home.

'Mm, he said it was important,' Merry said slowly.

'Even if it's only a small part——'

'Oh, it will be,' Merry smiled ruefully, feeling more comfortable in her denims and casual blouse.

'But just to work for Gideon Steele——'

'If he is Gideon Steele.' She picked up her shoulder-bag. 'Ready?'

Vanda followed her out of the theatre on their way to the Underground. 'You surely don't have any doubts about that?' she frowned.

'Well, Harry's hardly a good character witness,'

Merry derided. 'We all know Liam only got the male lead in the play because he's Harry's "friend".'

'But it *was* Gideon Steele. All six foot three, one hundred and seventy-five pounds, thirty-four years, black-haired, blue-eyed *bachelor* inch of him,' Vanda finished breathlessly.

'Know a bit about him, do you?' Merry teased.

'Not really,' her friend said tongue-in-cheek. 'His father is Samuel Steele, he owns one of the big airlines, I'm not sure which one. Well, I wasn't really interested in his father,' she protested at Merry's mischievous derision.

'Of course not.'

Vanda grinned, sitting beside her on the Underground train. 'He's really rich, you know.'

'The father or the son?' Merry mocked.

'Both. His father's loaded, but Gideon Steele is rich in his own right now. And his films speak for themselves.'

Yes, they did. After that first youthful mistake, they had all been masterpieces in their own way, and last year's Oscar had been well deserved. If she could get a part in one of his films her career could really take off—and in the right direction this time! The sooner this play was over and forgotten the better she would like it.

Vanda was of the same opinion. 'At least you're in with a chance,' she grimaced. 'I think it's back to the dole queue for me tomorrow.'

Merry's eyes widened. 'That soon?'

'In case you didn't notice, it was the critics who walked out first. This play will be heralded as Harry Anderson's biggest folly to date.'

And indeed it was! The critics ripped him and the play to pieces. In fact, they didn't have a good word to say for anyone in it either, although luckily no one was mentioned by name. When they turned up for rehearsal that morning it was to be told that 'Mr Anderson has decided to take a cruise on his yacht. For an indefinite period'. All the staff were paid off, and they were all out of work again.

Merry dressed carefully for her luncheon appointment, wanting to make a good impression now that she had checked and found that Gideon Steele was who he said he was. It wasn't too difficult to verify, he was a well-known personality in the crowd she mixed with, and it was rumoured that he *was* on the look-out for new talent for a film he intended doing later in the year.

She wished she hadn't been so presumptuous as to choose the Ritz, though. It had been a perverse act of defiance on her part, and it had backfired on her. It wasn't really her sort of place, not the pomp and ceremony, the snobbishness. Oh well, she would make the best of it. After all, she was an actress, wasn't she?

None of her nervousness showed as she was taken to Gideon Steele's table in the lounge area, and her red suit, the narrow skirt and blouson top, looked as good as any of the clothes the other women wore. Except the woman in the fur coat—and as she abhorred the killing of animals for furs, this really didn't count.

Gideon Steele stood up as she arrived at the table, easily the most impressive man in the room, his light grey three-piece suit and black shirt perfectly tailored, very expensive by the look of the cut, his tie a perfect match in colour for the suit. And today the tinted glasses had been removed, revealing very deep blue eyes surrounded by thick dark lashes, the face incredibly handsome in a rugged sort of way. Certainly handsome enough to star in one of his own films instead of just directing them!

If Merry was bowled over by his good looks he made

no effort to hide his surprise at hers. 'God . . .!' his eyes were intent on her face and hair as she sat down, sitting down himself once she had done so. 'I thought last night that the hair was yours!'

'Pink?' she derided with sarcasm, giving every impression of frequenting restaurants like this every day of her life.

He shrugged broad shoulders. 'It was possible. Women today seem to dye their hair to match the colour of their clothes.'

'I never wear black, Mr Steele,' she told him coldly. 'But my hair stays that colour.'

'And green eyes.' He shook his head. 'It's incredible!'

Those green eyes widened, the lashes thick and silky, naturally dark, the tips golden. 'There's nothing incredible about my colouring, Mr Steele.'

'Oh yes, there is,' he nodded, watching her with narrowed eyes. 'Let's go in to lunch and you can tell me about yourself.'

'There's nothing to tell,' she dismissed.

'Nevertheless, I want to hear it.' He stood up to pull back her chair for her, towering over her as they walked side by side into the dining-room, the walls lined with mirrors, the ceiling very ornate. Meredith had never been here before, and she found it all beautifully elegant.

For the next fifteen minutes she gave him a résumé of what she had been doing since she left school four years ago, hardly noticing the food that was quietly and efficiently placed in front of her, only knowing that it was delicious.

'And your family?' he prompted.

She frowned. 'Is that necessary?'

She couldn't see what her family history had to do with giving her a part in a film, but after the indifference she had treated him with the night before she was willing to do anything to please him. Well, not quite anything, she thought ruefully.

'Something funny?' He quirked one dark brow, perfectly relaxed with his surroundings, taking the efficiency of the service for granted, the perfection of the food.

And also the female attention coming his way. And there was plenty of that! Young and old alike seemed to feel his magnetism, the aura of sensuality that Merry was becoming more and more aware of with each sip of wine.

'Not really,' she smiled. 'It was really good of you to agree to meet me here. You must have thought me very audacious yesterday.'

'Possibly,' he replied enigmatically, dismissively. 'You were going to tell me about your family.'

She looked at him over the rim of her glass. 'What would you like to know?'

He sat forward, his expression intent. 'Everything.'

'What an invitation!' she laughed huskily. 'I'm sure you don't mean "everything"?'

'My dear Miss Charles,' he drawled with barely concealed impatience, 'I never do, or say, anything I don't mean.'

'How clever of you!' her sarcasm was barely veiled.

'Yes,' he agreed tersely.

'Don't you know that it's fatal to invite an actor or actress to talk about his or herself? I could go on for hours,' she warned lightly.

'I'm willing to take the risk,' he taunted, the blue eyes deeply mocking.

'All right,' Merry sighed. 'I've lived a very normal life, with very normal parents.'

He scowled at her, the black brows dark over his eyes. 'That was hardly hours,' he snapped.

'I can't help that,' she shrugged. 'That's been my life so far. I've lived a very uneventful life. In fact,' she added softly, 'the most exciting thing to happen to me so far is meeting you.' Her eyes were widely innocent.

His mouth twisted with scepticism. 'I don't need flattery, Miss Charles,' he rasped. 'Especially the insincere kind.'

She flushed at the way he had seen straight through her. So much for her acting! He was right, her flattery was insincere. Something about this man warned her to beware, that he was dangerous. Maybe it was the way he kept staring at her, those deep blue eyes totally unnerving, making her wish he had kept the tinted glasses on. Whatever the reason for her nervousness, she knew that here was a man she could never relax with, and her guard was well and truly up—although she had nothing to hide.

'Do you still live with your parents?' he asked now.

She shook her head. 'My father lives in Bedfordshire. I have to live in London for my work.'

'And your mother?'

A flicker of pain crossed her face. 'She died, two years ago,' she revealed huskily.

Gideon Steele nodded. 'I didn't think there'd been any mistake. The moment I saw you today, without the wig and that atrocious make-up, I knew Harrington hadn't been wrong about you. But I had to be sure.'

'Sure of what?' Merry frowned, suddenly tense. 'And who is Harrington?'

'That isn't important for now,' he dismissed impatiently. 'What is important is that Anthea sees you straight away.'

'Who is Anthea? Your casting director?'

'Don't be ridiculous! Anthea is——' he broke off with a frown. 'Why did you think I wanted to meet you today?' he asked slowly.

'Well, everyone knows you're in town looking for people for your next film, and——'

'You thought I was going to cast you?' he finished incredulously.

She flushed resentfully. 'Why else would you want to see me?'

'Because of your mother,' he rasped. 'Good God, girl, you could be a brilliant actress for all I know, but I certainly wouldn't have been able to tell from Anderson's play.'

'That isn't the only thing I've been in,' she defended heatedly, her disappointment acute. He wasn't going to offer her a part after all. 'And what does my mother have to do with you? I told you, she's dead.' Her voice shook with emotion.

'You told me Sarah Charles is dead——'

'That is my mother. And how did you know her name?' Her voice was sharp with suspicion. 'I didn't tell you.'

'I already knew it. I also know your father's name is Malcolm, that you were born on April the fourteenth twenty years ago, that you had a boy-friend called David——'

'How do you know all that?' she gasped, her glass landing heavily on the table, unconcerned with the curious glances now coming their way. 'Why did you *need* to know that? You had no right going into my background!'

'I had every right,' he told her abruptly. 'You see, I'm your stepbrother. Your mother is married to my father.'

Merry paled. 'My mother is dead,' she said weakly. 'I just told you that.'

He gave her an impatient look. 'I meant your real mother——'

'*Real* mother?' she echoed shrilly, her eyes huge in her pale face. 'I don't know what you mean!'

'Perhaps we should get out of here and go somewhere

where we can talk more privately?' he suggested abruptly, signalling the waiter for their bill.

Merry's movements were jerky as she picked up her handbag. 'We have nothing more to say to each other.'

'Meredith——'

'Take your hands off me!' She wrenched away from him. 'You got me here under the pretence of offering me a part in your film——'

'I didn't,' he sighed. 'You surmised that all on your own.'

'What else was I supposed to think?' Her eyes flashed deeply green. 'I had no idea you had some sort of dossier on me!'

'Meredith, you have to listen,' his expression was intent, the jaw rigid. 'Anthea wants to see you.'

'*Who* is Anthea?' she cried her bewilderment, wondering if this man were deranged.

'Your mother.'

'My mother's name was Sarah—Sarah Charles!' she told him heatedly.

He gave an angry sigh. 'You aren't helping matters by this ridiculous refusal to admit the truth. You may have thought of Sarah Charles as your mother, and I'm sure she was a very good one, but that doesn't change the fact that Anthea, my stepmother, is really your mother, that the Charleses adopted you when you were only a few months old. I realise it must have been painful for you to accept when you were a child, but surely by this time you're used to it?'

Merry shook her head dazedly, unable to hide her distress. 'You were wrong about me, Mr Steele. I'm not the girl you were looking for after all. My name is Meredith Charles, yes, and my parents' names are Sarah and Malcolm, but I—I wasn't adopted.' Her voice shook.

'Meredith——'

She stood up. 'You have the wrong girl, Mr Steele,' she told him hardly. 'The wrong girl!' She turned away, walking straight into the waiter bringing their bill, pushing past him with a muttered apology, almost running out of the restaurant, knowing that Gideon Steele couldn't follow her when he had to pay the bill.

But why should he want to follow her? He had the wrong Meredith Charles, the wrong person completely. He had to have! She couldn't possibly be the daughter of some woman called Anthea. Her mother was Sarah Charles. She was!

CHAPTER TWO

'HEY, how did—Merry?' Vanda frowned as Merry rushed straight past her into her bedroom, closing the door behind her. 'Merry?' Vanda knocked on the door anxiously. 'What happened? Was it just an approach after all?' Anger entered her voice.

Merry sat numbly on the bedroom chair, her thoughts racing—and all of them telling her it had all been a terrible mistake, that what Gideon Steele had told her couldn't possibly be true of *her*!

'Merry, can I come in?' Vanda requested gently, softly opening the door as she received no answer. 'Oh, love!' she groaned as she saw Merry's pale face, coming down on her knees in front of the chair. 'What did he do to you?'

'Do?' Merry repeated dazedly. 'Nothing. He didn't do anything to me.'

'Then why—Damn!' Vanda swore as the doorbell rang, standing up to go and answer it.

Merry looked panic-stricken. 'I don't want to see him. I *won't* see him!'

'All right, love,' the other girl soothed. 'I'll tell him you haven't got back yet. I'm not an actress for nothing!' She closed the bedroom door firmly behind her, a determined glint in her eyes.

Merry heard the flat door being opened, the murmur of voices, and then silence. She would never be able to thank Vanda enough for getting rid of Gideon Steele. She needed time to think right now, to get her thoughts together—to forget what he had told her.

She looked down at the carpet as the bedroom door opened once more. 'Thanks, Vanda,' she murmured. 'I didn't want to talk to him again. You see, he has some wild story——'

'It isn't wild, Meredith,' his husky voice interrupted her.

'You!' she gasped, looking up at Gideon Steele with wide green eyes, her hands clutching convulsively at the arms of the chair. Vanda hadn't managed to put him off after all!

'Yes,' he sighed wearily, slightly pale beneath his tan. 'Can I talk to you?'

She doubted this man requested very often, he was the type who did things without asking anyone's permission. But she didn't feel in the least warmed by the fact that he was asking her now. What he had done to her had been cruel and thoughtless. He should have made sure of his facts before confronting her with such a ridiculous story. As it was, she was in no mood to listen to anything further he might have to say.

Some of what she was thinking must have shown in her face. 'I think we have to, Meredith,' he encouraged softly, closing the door behind him.

Her head went back, her eyes defiant. 'If you want to apologise——'

He shook his head. 'I can't apologise for telling the truth. I can apologise for the *way* I told you. I had no idea you didn't know about your adoption.'

She stood up, moving about the room with agitated movements. 'I wish you'd stop saying that,' she snapped. 'You can't know how wrong you are,' she gave a scornful laugh. 'I'm so like my father that what you're telling me is ridiculous. Ever since I can remember people have remarked on the similarity.'

His hands were thrust into his trousers pockets, his height dwarfing the tiny bedroom. 'Maybe they were just being kind—or maybe you do have the same colouring.' He shrugged. 'I've heard that adoption societies try to do that, match the child up with at least one of the parents. Any facial similarity would have to be a coincidence,' he shook his head. 'I've never seen two people more alike than you and Anthea.'

'Your stepmother,' she said bitterly.

'That's right,' he nodded grimly. 'When you walked into the restaurant today it was like seeing Anthea as she must have looked twenty years ago.'

'Maybe I do bear some resemblance to this woman——'

'It isn't just a resemblance, Meredith,' Gideon Steele shook his head. 'Look, I can show you a photograph if you like,' his hand went into the breast pocket of his jacket.

'No!' she stopped him in the action of taking out his wallet. 'I don't want to see any photograph.' She turned away, absently twisting the signet ring round on her right hand, the ring that had been a birthday gift several years ago from her parents. 'It won't make any difference,' she told him stiffly.

'Scared, Meredith?' he taunted gruffly.

'Certainly not!' She spun round, an angry frown between her eyes. 'I have nothing to be frightened of,' she said haughtily. 'It's quite simple, you have the wrong girl,' she repeated her earlier claim.

'The right one,' he corrected softly, running an agitated hand through the darkness of his hair, revealing several streaks of grey beneath the darkness. 'God, I had no idea it was going to be this difficult!' he scowled.

'What did you expect?' Merry shouted angrily. 'That you could calmly walk up to some unsuspecting girl and tell her that her parents aren't her parents any more, and that some unknown woman *is*? If you thought that you're a fool!'

'Meredith——' he began warningly.

'I don't care,' she exclaimed furiously. 'You had no right barging into my life with such a story! If I were of a nervous disposition——'

'Which you obviously aren't,' he drawled hardly.

'Luckily for you,' she snapped. 'But if I were I could have been totally destroyed by what you just told me. As it is, I think you'd better go back to your source— Harrington, I presume,' she added drily. 'And tell him it's back to the drawing-board. Why do you want to find this girl anyway? Has your stepmother died and left her the family fortune?'

His mouth twisted derisively. 'Would it change your mind if she had?' he taunted.

She gave an angry gasp. 'How dare you! I have no intention——'

'Calm down, Meredith,' he mocked. 'Anthea is still very much alive. She would just like to see her daughter.'

'Whom she abandoned as a baby, by the sound of it!'

If she had expected an angry defence to her scorn she was mistaken, Gideon Steele only nodded abruptly. 'Anthea hasn't denied that. But it hasn't stopped her feeling guilty for the last twenty years, for wanting to see her daughter.'

'Has she ever stopped to consider that perhaps her daughter doesn't want to see her?' Merry snapped.

'I only said she wanted to see her daughter, I didn't say she had made any attempt to do so. My stepmother has no idea I've sought you out. She certainly doesn't know I've found you.'

'But I keep telling you you haven't,' she said exasperatedly.

His mouth was a thin determined line. 'There's a sure way of settling this, Meredith——'

'Please call me Merry,' she invited irritably. 'I prefer it. And how can this be settled?'

'Talk to your father——'

'No!' she almost shouted, glaring at him.

'Then you are frightened——'

'I am not!' she snapped. 'I just don't think it's fair to put something like that to my father. He's never really got over losing my mother, all he needs is my asking him if he's really my father!' She gave Gideon Steele a disgusted look. 'I won't do that to him.'

'Then take my word for it——'

'I won't do that either,' she told him coldly, giving the impression she would never take *his* word for anything. 'I've already told you, I'm not the girl you're looking for, so why don't you leave me alone?'

'Ordinarily I wouldn't have bothered to find you in the first place,' he said harshly. 'Anthea's past is her own affair—and my father's if she chooses to tell him about it. But she told us both about you last year.'

'Why?' Merry frowned.

'If you aren't her daughter why are you interested?' His eyes were narrowed.

She flushed. 'You involved me in this, I just wanted to know all the facts.'

'If you aren't the Meredith Charles I'm looking for then I don't see the necessity of acquainting you with them.' He moved to the door. 'As you suggested, I'll go back to my source. And I suggest *you* go to your father.'

'I——'

'I'll be back, Meredith,' he warned. 'And if necessary, I'll bring Harrington *and* the dossier to prove the truth to you.' He swung the door open. 'I'd advise you to be prepared. Go and see your father, Meredith,' he said softly. 'After all, what real harm can it do? I'm sure there must be some way you can ask Malcolm Charles if he is your father without being blunt about it. I'll be seeing you, Meredith,' he promised before leaving.

'I'm so sorry,' Vanda hurried into the room as soon as Gideon Steele had left the apartment, 'but he just wouldn't take no for an answer.' She grimaced. 'And he isn't the sort of man you can argue with.'

'No,' she agreed vaguely, pulling her suitcase down from the top of the wardrobe. 'I'm going to see my father for a few days, Vanda. I—If Mr Steele should come back, you don't know where I've gone, all right?'

'Are you that frightened of him?' Vanda asked in an awed voice.

She gave a taut smile. 'I'm not frightened of him. I just—I don't like him.' And she didn't, she didn't like his self-assurance, his arrogance—and most of all she didn't like the things he had told her.

'He didn't offer you a part, then?' Vanda sat on the bed as she watched Merry pack.

Only that of his stepsister, she thought hysterically. It was unthinkable that a man like that should be any sort of relative of hers, no matter how remote. 'No,' she answered calmly enough. 'And as the play has folded I thought I'd go and see Dad for a few days. He gets a little lonely without my mother.'

In fact her father seemed sprightlier than ever. His job in the nearest town at the branch of one of the countries leading insurance agencies kept him very busy, filling most of his evenings at least.

He met her at the station, hugging her before taking her case out to the car. 'I couldn't believe it when I got your call,' he smiled at her, his hair still as black as her own, his eyes more hazel than green; he was still a very handsome man, despite being in his late forties.

Merry listened to all his chatter about the locals in the little village she had lived in most of her life, knowing all the two hundred or so inhabitants by name, and most of their pets too! After the impersonality of London it always warmed her to return to Wildton, and she waved to several of the neighbours children as they played in their gardens.

'Nothing's changed,' she said with pleasure as she followed her father into the small bungalow that seemed so empty without her mother's bustling presence in the kitchen.

'You have,' her father said softly, putting her case in her room, filled with the posters of pop stars she had put up when in her teens still on the walls, the patchwork quilt on the bed, the bookcase full of the romance novels she still devoured by their hundreds, an old guitar propped in the corner of the room.

She looked sharply at her father. 'What do you mean?'

He shrugged, a sad smile to his handsome face. 'When you left two years ago you were still a little girl, now you suddenly seem grown up.'

Merry's bottom lip quivered, and suddenly she was in his arms, sobbing into his shoulder as if she would never stop. She felt safe in her father's arms, safe and secure, with Gideon Steele pushed firmly to the back of her mind.

'Hey!' her father finally chided, holding her at arm's

length. 'Surely growing up isn't that painful?' he teased, his gentle strength comforting her.

'I'm afraid it is.' She wiped her cheeks with the handkerchief he gave her, her smile rather weak.

'A man?' he prompted softly.

'I—Yes,' she decided, knowing the truth was too much to even think about. 'A man.'

'Now I definitely feel old,' he smiled. 'My daughter's first unhappy love affair!'

'Oh, Dad!' she sniffed, smiling broadly. Everything seemed so normal when she was with her father, when she could feel his love, could see their similarity in looks, that Gideon Steele's suggestion now seemed as ludicrous as she had said it was. Seeing her father's gentle love for her she was ashamed of ever doubting him.

It was an enjoyable time at home, and yet she was aware of a subtle difference in her own behaviour. She was unsettled, irritable, and it wasn't just because of her lack of a job when she returned to London. She found herself watching her father with a keenness she had never felt before, felt anger at herself for noticing that the similarity between them was only superficial, their colouring going a long way towards giving the impression of father and daughter. There was also the fact that both her parents were tall. She had always credited her own diminutive height to one of her grandmothers, but now she had an uneasy feeling inside her. She was starting to believe Gideon Steele's fantastic claim!

The day she came home from an afternoon's shopping and found him sitting in the lounge with her father she knew that he, at least, was convinced there was nothing fantastic about it.

'A friend of yours from London,' her father smiled as she came in, carrying two cans of beer through to the lounge.

Merry wouldn't, even in her wildest dreams, ever call Gideon Steele a friend. Although he gave every indication of being one as he stood up to greet her.

'Meridith!' He gave her a warm smile, accepting one of the cans of beer from her father. 'Thanks,' he accepted gratefully, turning back to Merry. 'I've just been telling your father how we met.'

She swallowed hard. 'You have?'

She had known he was here before she entered the house, had seen the Ferrari outside and knew no one else could own that black monster. He was several inches taller than her father, more powerfully built, and looked extremely fit in the fitted black shirt and black trousers. He seemed to dominate the whole room—and the people in it!

'Yes,' he continued to smile. 'It's the only good thing Harry Anderson has ever done in his life, I should think.'

'Harry?' she echoed sharply, wondering what on earth he had been telling her father. Of course, her father already knew about Harry, she had told him all about the disastrous play. But what could Harry possibly have to do with Gideon Steele and herself?

'He sounds an atrocious person,' her father grinned.

'Oh, he is,' Gideon nodded. 'Not the sort of man Meredith should associate herself with.'

'I——'

'And a waste of her acting talent,' he added softly, eyeing her mockingly as he drank the beer straight from the can with obvious enjoyment.

'Really, I don't——'

'I'd better get going.' Her father looked at his wristwatch. 'Time for work, I'm afraid,' he told Gideon ruefully.

The other man nodded. 'I understand.'

And Merry knew how he understood! If he had

done enough research on her to know her background then he also knew that her father was an insurance agent, that he spent most of his evenings visiting clients, usually able to catch people in at that time of day.

'I'm sure Merry will be pleased to get you some dinner,' her father continued goodnaturedly. 'I've had mine, love,' he kissed her absently on the cheek. 'See you later. You too, I hope, Gideon?'

Merry looked sharply at Gideon Steele. It hadn't taken her father and him long to get on to a first-name basis. And there was still the puzzle of what he had told her father about how they met.

'I'm not sure yet, Malcolm,' he answered easily, his gaze firmly fixed on Merry.

'I understand,' her father nodded. 'Don't be too hard on him, pet,' he advised Merry before leaving the room.

Colour flooded her cheeks at the assumption her father had made that Gideon Steele was the man from her 'first unhappy love affair', and her blushes deepened as she saw the derision in Gideon Steele's eyes.

'What are you doing here?' she snapped ungraciously.

He shrugged and sat down again, perfectly relaxed. 'I told you I'd be back once I was sure of my facts.'

Her breath caught in her throat. 'And now you are?'

'I'm sorry, Merry, but yes, I am.'

There was no doubting his sympathy, or the look of regret in the deep blue eyes, and the emotions sat strangely on such a harshly determined man.

He stood up to pace the room, having discarded the empty beer can in the bin. 'I went back to Harrington, told him to check on all the facts. They led straight back to you, Merry. I really am sorry,' he repeated deeply. 'I gather you haven't spoken to your father?'

'No! And I'm not going to,' she added fiercely.

'But you do believe me?' he prompted softly.

She wetted her suddenly dry lips with the tip of her

tongue, wishing she could say no, but knowing it would be a lie. A man like Gideon Steele was unlikely to be wrong once, let alone twice! If he said she was adopted, that her mother was really his stepmother Anthea, then she had to believe him. But it changed nothing for her, made no difference to the love she felt for her parents. Anthea Steele had given her up when she was a baby, so she had no claims on her now, moral or otherwise.

'Yes, I believe you,' she answered in a cold voice.

'So you'll come and see Anthea?'

'No.'

'Good God, girl——! She's your mother!' he ground out, his mouth a thin angry line, the tautness of his body telling her of the control he was exerting. 'She brought you into the world——'

'And just as soon deserted me, by the sound of it!' Her eyes glittered deeply green in her own anger.

'She was very young, she's only thirty-eight now——'

'I don't care how old she was. She gave me up, she can't come along twenty years later and try to claim a family love. It would be disloyal to my father to even acknowledge her existence.'

Gideon Steele shook his head. 'I'm sure you're doing your father an injustice. He seems a very reasonable man.'

'Whether he is or not is not a subject for discussion.'

'Drop that haughty act with me, Merry——'

'It isn't an act, Mr Steele,' she snapped. 'I am not interested in meeting your stepmother, because as far as I'm concerned that's all she is. My own mother paced the floor with me as a baby, fretted for me when I started school, worried about me when I was ill, encouraged me through my exams, waited up for me on my first date, celebrated with me when I got into drama school. Can your stepmother do any of that?' Her scorn was unmistakable.

Gideon Steele drew in an angry breath, a pulse beating erratically in his lean cheek, his shirt pulled tautly across his chest as he thrust his hands into the back pockets of his trousers. He looked lean and powerful in that moment—a man far from beaten in this argument.

'I'm not suggesting you welcome her with open arms,' he rasped. 'Or that she could ever take the place of your adoptive mother——'

'She never could!'

He looked impatient with her vehemence. 'As I said,' he drawled hardly, 'I'm not suggesting that. What I *am* saying is that maybe you could be friends. Anthea would like that,' he added softly.

Merry studied his softened expression with suspicion. Could he possibly feel more than a maternal love for his stepmother? He said Anthea was thirty-eight, that made her only four years older than he was, and it also made his father a lot older than his wife.

'Did she marry your father for his money?' she asked suspiciously.

His mouth tightened. 'What sort of question is that?' Anger oozed out of him.

Her head went back. 'Did she?'

'They've been married for twelve years,' he revealed abruptly. 'I think my father would have realised by now if that were the case.'

'Twelve years?' she repeated softly. 'Then she's had all that time to think about wanting to know her daughter, so why now? Why doesn't she just have another child and forget all about me?'

'I'm beginning to think she would be better doing that myself!' he rasped.

Merry flushed at his rebuke. 'I'm sure she would.'

'And will you forget her too?' he taunted harshly. 'Don't be stupid, Merry. Now that you know of her existence it would be impossible to ignore her. As for why she would want to see you now, I can tell you that she's always wanted to see you, but that she tried to be fair to you and not interfere in your life while you were still a child.' His derisive expression showed that he still thought that was so. 'Last year, when she was in hospital, she told us about you. I think she just wanted us to know that she had a daughter, a daughter she loved.'

'In hospital?' Merry repeated sharply. 'What's wrong with her?'

'Why are you interested?' he mocked.

Merry glared at him. 'I'm not——'

'She had a nervous breakdown,' he cut in steadily. 'She'd been living on her nerves for years, and she just suddenly folded up. We finally discovered it was because of you, because of the guilt she still felt for giving you up.'

'But that was last year?' she frowned. 'Surely she's well now?'

He sighed. 'Surperficially, yes. But she's been on pills ever since, and my father fears that she'll have another breakdown.'

Her mouth twisted. 'Wouldn't producing me give her rather a shock? You said she knows nothing of your search for me?'

'I wish I could believe your concern for her was genuine,' he snapped angrily. 'But I know damn well it isn't.' He took a card out of his breast pocket and wrote on the back of it. 'If you ever find yourself with a little compassion to spare call me at this number. But don't call me otherwise,' he rasped. 'Anthea couldn't cope with your derision and hate. Now walk me to the door, like the polite little girl you've obviously been brought up to be,' he derided hardly, throwing the card down on the coffee table and following her out of the room.

Merry faced him awkwardly at the door, his contempt for her not missing its target.

'Think it over carefully, Merry,' he turned to warn her. 'You could be turning away the love of a woman who needs you, much more than you realise.'

'She has your father, she has you,' she told him coldly. 'I can't see any possible reason for her needing me, a child she hasn't seen for twenty years.'

His eyes were glacial. 'Can't you?' he rasped coldly. 'Then your adoptive parents have failed you.'

'How dare——'

'They haven't taught you forgiveness,' he cut into her anger. 'Goodbye, Meredith. I hoped it wouldn't be like this.' He shook his head. 'I'm sorry.'

She closed the door as he left, but she didn't move herself. She knew that his regret hadn't been because he had come here to confirm what he had told her four days ago, she knew it was because he was disappointed in her lack of maturity in *accepting* what he had told her.

'He's wrong, isn't he, Merry?' her father questioned quietly behind her.

She spun round, guilty colour flooding her cheeks as she saw her father sitting down partway up the stairs. 'You heard . . .?'

'All of it,' he nodded. 'I came back for some papers I'd forgotten. I overheard—I couldn't help but listen.'

She swallowed hard. 'Is it true?'

Again he nodded. 'He was wrong, wasn't he, Merry?' he persisted. 'Your mother and I did teach you forgiveness, didn't we?'

It was a double-edged question, and she knew he was asking for forgiveness for himself as much as for Anthea Steele. 'Oh, Dad!' She ran to him, the tears falling unchecked down her cheeks as she threw herself into his arms.

For a moment he just held her, letting her cry, stroking her hair as he had done when she was a child and needed comforting. 'It's all right, baby,' he finally spoke to her, his own voice thick with emotion. 'And you are still my baby, Merry, no matter who brought you into this world.'

She looked up at him with shadowed eyes. 'Why . . .?'

'I know,' he sighed. 'We should have told you when you were still a child, but we kept putting it off, and putting it off, keeping you as our very own little girl, I think. Then we decided that your eighteenth birthday would be time enough to tell you, when you were old enough to understand that we loved you even though we hadn't managed to conceive you. But you know what happened just before your birthday,' he added sadly.

'Mummy died,' Merry said shakily, the memory of the horror of that night three weeks before her eighteenth birthday still as vivid. Her mother had been knocked over by a car and killed.

'Yes,' her father acknowledged heavily. 'After that I couldn't tell you, didn't have the courage to without your mother. But you are still our daughter, Merry,' he told her firmly.

'That's what I told Gideon Steele——'

'But you do have a real mother,' he continued as if she hadn't spoken. 'And right now she sounds as if she needs you. Your mother did all the things for you that you claimed she did, and that forged a bond of love between you that's so strong it will never be broken. But she *didn't* bring you into the world, that was left to some other woman—to Anthea Steele.'

'But——'

'Let me finish, Merry,' he spoke strongly. 'Your mother and I love you, you know we always will.

Gideon's stepmother, your real mother, could only have been seventeen when she became pregnant with you. Seventeen, Merry! Do you remember what you felt like at that age—imagine the trauma of expecting a baby when you were no more than a child yourself?'

She thought back to when she had been seventeen, to when she had been in her last year at school, taking her 'A' levels. She couldn't have coped with a baby at that age.

'You see?' her father prompted gently as he watched the different emotions flickering across her face.

Merry remained adamant. 'Then she shouldn't have got pregnant! She——'

'If she hadn't your mother and I would never have had you to love,' he pointed out softly. 'Your mother had every test possible, and she couldn't have children of her own. Adoption was our only way of ever having a child then. If it weren't for Anthea Steele, we would never have had you as our daughter.'

Hurt still warred with reason, her pain reflected in her deep green eyes.

'I think Mrs Steele needs you, Merry,' her father said softly. 'I think she's needed you for some time, for her sanity.'

Fresh tears flooded her eyes, falling softly down her pale cheeks, confusion, and also a reluctant curiosity, reflected in her eyes.

Her father was quick to note the latter emotion, and nodded slowly. 'No matter what happens you'll always be our daughter,' he assured her intently. 'But I don't feel it would be disloyal to me to see your real mother. In fact, I'd feel rather proud if you did.'

'P-proud?' she repeated shakily.

He smiled. 'If I do say so myself, we've done rather a nice job of bringing you up. I'd like Mrs Steele to see that her sacrifice wasn't for nothing.'

Merry frowned once again at his choice of words. 'Sacrifice?'

Her father nodded. 'You don't think she found it easy to give you up, do you? Because it wasn't,' he shook his head. 'No woman could give her child up without causing herself pain. And it's a pain that has obviously never left Anthea Steele.' He stood up, taking Merry with him. 'Think about it, darling,' he advised. 'I'm not pressurising you to see her if you really don't think you could cope with it, but I would be very pleased if you could. All right?'

'All right,' she nodded tearfully, once again thinking what a wonderful man her father was.

He smiled, wiping away her tears. 'The stairs is a ridiculous place to have had this conversation,' his smile deepened to a grin, 'but I'm glad we've had it.'

'So am I,' Merry said, and meant it, giving him a quick kiss and a hug before running up the stairs to her bedroom.

A few minutes later she heard the front door close, and knew that her father had gone to work as usual. She could hear the local children playing outside as usual, the occasional car as usual. Only she seemed to have changed. She was no longer just the daughter of Sarah and Malcolm Charles, she was also the daughter of Anthea Steele, the stepdaughter of Samuel Steele, and stepsister to Gideon Steele. Just knowing that changed the whole fabric of her life, made her want to know *exactly* who she was, and what Anthea Steele was really like.

But she didn't run headlong into meeting her real mother. She gave herself time to think, to consider the consequences of such a meeting, for them both. For herself she didn't feel she would be too deeply affected if such a meeting didn't work out—after all, she still had her father, no matter what. But if Anthea Steele were in the emotional depression her stepson claimed she was then it could have a disastrous effect on her.

Finally it was the curiosity that made her seek out Gideon Steele at the telephone number he had given her. It turned out to be a hotel, and it took several minutes to put through to his room. When there was no answer the hotel telephonist came back on the line.

'Could I take a message for Mr Steele?' she offered politely.

Merry chewed on her bottom lip, not sure she would be able to find the courage to call Gideon Steele again. 'Could you tell him Miss Charles called,' she said breathlessly.

Now if he still wanted her to meet his stepmother it would be up to him to contact her! Nevertheless, she made the concession of turning down the invitation Vanda passed on about a party at one of their friends' flats. After all, there was no point in leaving a message that she had called him if she then went out for the evening herself.

By ten o'clock she was beginning to wish she had gone with Vanda; the lateness of the hour seemed to indicate that Gideon Steele had gone out for the entire evening too.

She was in the process of changing to go to the party after all when the doorbell rang. She zipped up her skin-tight red velvet trousers as she ran to answer the door, her red and gold interwoven top also figure-hugging.

Her eyes widened as she found Gideon Steele standing outside the door. Once again his suit was superbly tailored, blue this time, contrasted with a lighter blue shirt, and there was a weary look about his eyes and mouth as he raised dark brows at her appearance.

'Mr Steele . . .' she said weakly.

'You called me——'

'I expected you to *call* back, not just turn up here!' She was instantly on the defensive, something about this autocratic man making her feel that way whenever she met him. 'I was just on my way out.'

'And I thought the outfit was for my benefit,' he drawled.

Merry flushed. 'Hardly!'

He gave an impatient sigh, his face darkening to a scowl. 'Could we talk about this inside?' he snapped.

She opened the door to him warily, taking her time about closing it again, allowing herself time to collect her thoughts together. Why couldn't he have just telephoned her? It would have been so much easier talking to him on the telephone, to have agreed to meet Anthea Steele if she hadn't had to speak to him face to face. She wouldn't put it past this arrogant devil of a man to know that, after all, he must know the reason she had called him. There could only be one reason!

He was waiting for her in the lounge, his impatience barely concealed as he tapped his fingers on the old stone fireplace that now housed an electric fire, drawing attention to the artistic sensitivity of his hands.

'I'm to take it you've changed your mind about meeting Anthea?' He finally spoke, impatient with her silence.

Dull colour flooded her cheeks at his directness. 'Yes,' she bit out.

He nodded, as if she could make no other answer. 'You've spoken with your father?'

'Yes.'

His scowl deepened. 'Aren't you going to say anything else but "yes"?' he snapped tersely.

Merry shrugged. 'There isn't anything else to say, you seem to know all the answers.'

He raised his eyes heavenwards. 'Does that mean you can't at least make a token show at conversation?'

She flushed at his rebuke. 'It's all been said. I've spoken to my father, we've agreed that it isn't disloyal to him and my mother if I meet my—your stepmother.' She bit her lip at the angry flare in his eyes as she corrected herself. Anthea Steele *wasn't* her mother, and never could be.

'Very well,' Gideon Steele rasped tautly. 'When do you want to meet her?' His eyes were narrowed.

'I—I haven't really thought about it.' The decision to see her at all had been hard enough. 'When do you think . . .?'

'There's no time like the present——'

'Not now!' Merry gasped her protest. 'Not tonight. It's ten-thirty!'

'So late!' he taunted mockingly. 'You've just admitted that you were on your way out, so it isn't that late after all. But as it happens, I didn't have right now in mind. I think tomorrow would be a good time.'

It was all happening too fast, was like a snowball rolling down a hillside, getting bigger and bigger as it went—and it threatened to knock her off her feet when it came to an end!

'Too soon?'

It was the taunting softness of his voice that brought the spark of rebellion into her glittering green eyes. 'Of course not,' she answered lightly. 'Tomorrow will be fine.'

'Good,' he nodded his satisfaction, his expression grim. 'Do you have a valid passport?'

Merry blinked dazedly. 'Passport?' she repeated incredulously, not able to keep up with his lightning change of subjects.

'Yes. Do you?' his impatience was barely contained.

She frowned. 'As it happens, yes. I went to Austria with some friends last year. Why do I need a passport?'

'Anthea and my father are in the middle of a Mediterranean cruise at this moment. Tomorrow morning I'm on my way to join them for the last two weeks. You may as well come with me and meet Anthea then.'

'Oh, but—I can't—That's ridiculous!' she protested. 'I can't just up and leave tomorrow morning for two weeks!'

'Why not?' he queried softly. 'You aren't back in work yet, I already checked that out. Your father wouldn't mind, and you've already agreed to meet Anthea. So what's your problem?' he raised dark brows over eyes the colour of a storm-tossed sea, supremely confident, not understanding that although he might live the jet-set life that *she* didn't. She couldn't possibly just go off with him *tomorrow* to heaven alone knew where!

'*You*'re the problem,' she told him heatedly. 'Expecting me to just up and leave at a moment's notice for—for——'

'Athens,' he supplied calmly.

'Athens,' she repeated pointedly. 'I can't just——'

'Why not?' he interrupted.

'Well, because—I just can't! I don't have a seat booked on the plane——'

'It's a private jet.'

'I'm not booked on the ship——'

'It's family owned, there's always room for the family—and friends,' he added with a drawl.

So Vanda had got it wrong, it was shipping the Steele family were involved in—or was it shipping *and* airlines? He said it was a private jet. Probably both, she thought ruefully.

'Settled?' he taunted.

She could think of no further objections to make, and her mouth set in a thin disapproving line.

'The ship will be an easier place for you and Anthea to become acquainted,' he continued at her silence. 'It will be more relaxing for you both.'

'You think so?' she said stiffly, knowing that at any other time she would have been thrilled at the idea of a Mediterranean cruise. But not in these circumstances.

His icy blue gaze raked over her. 'I'm hoping so,' he said pointedly. 'On the way over here I also gave the problem of upsetting Anthea some thought.'

'Yes?' For some reason she suddenly felt wary.

'You were right about it being a shock for her to have you suddenly produced before her. That wouldn't be a good idea. My proposal is that you become my girl-friend for two weeks so that you can get to know each other naturally.'

CHAPTER THREE

'IT will never work,' Merry was still protesting at such an idea as they drove to the airport the next morning. Although the very fact that she was seated next to Gideon Steele in the sleek Ferrari proved that her protests were only token ones. She knew it, and so did Gideon Steele.

He quirked one dark brow at her. Today he was dressed casually in tight black denims and a black sweat-shirt. He looked ruggedly self-assured, and acted it too. 'I'll admit you're nothing like the women I usually have in my life,' he drawled. 'With one rather obvious disadvantage. Although there are plenty of others I can think of,' he added dryly.

Merry bristled angrily. 'Such as?' she prompted softly.

He stared grimly at the road in front of him, driving with the minimum of effort, relaxed to the point of laziness. 'You have a fiery temper,' he told her, just as if he were discussing something as innocuous as the weather. 'You're stubborn. And you're full of resentment towards me still.'

'And that's just the *minor* disadvantages!' she snapped. 'What's the main one?'

He gave a fleeting glance in her direction, seeming to take in everything about her, the long gleaming ebony hair, the light make-up that emphasised her high cheekbones and luminous green eyes, the light green tee-shirt that clung to the bareness of her breasts, the fashionably skin-tight denims, her feet thrust into rope sandals. She looked exactly what she was supposed to look, a girl going on holiday. So why was Gideon Steele looking at her like that?

'Your youth,' he stated bluntly, his haughty features appearing as if carved from granite in profile. 'I'm thirty-four, and I've never taken out a twenty-year-old!'

'Except when you were twenty!'

'Not even then.' He ignored her sarcasm, and shrugged. 'I've always preferred women in their thirties, women who know what they want from life, and don't confuse that wanting with love and romance.' His derision was obvious.

'You're talking about sex,' Merry stated disgustedly.

'Yes.'

She looked at him with rebellious green eyes. 'Maybe you should try looking at this from my point of view,' she said softly, too softly if he did but realise it.

He didn't. 'In what way?'

'That you have one *main* disadvantage that I don't like either.'

'Oh yes?' he prompted warily, sensing her challenge now.

'Yes,' she gave him a too-sweet smile. 'With the stupidity of youth,' she mocked, 'I happen to believe in love and romance. A middle-aged cynic like you wouldn't normally appeal to me at all!'

There were several minutes stunned silence after this taunting statement, and Merry found herself holding her breath as she waited for his reaction. Suddenly Gideon began to chuckle, a soft throaty sound that developed into a laugh of pure enjoyment.

'I forgot one thing in that list of disadvantages,' he still smiled. 'You're blunt to the point of rudeness.'

She shrugged, relieved that he hadn't exploded at her audacity. 'So are you.'

He turned to include her in his smile, the devastation of blue eyes crinkled at the corners, laughter lines beside his nose and mouth, his teeth very white against his tanned skin, knocking the breath from her body. 'Would you like to start again, Meredith?' he queried softly.

At last her breath returned to her, her lungs seeming to be starved of oxygen as she realised just how lethal this man could be if he ever stopped thinking of her as a child. Although that wasn't very likely!

'We could try,' she answered cagily, not sure it was possible for any woman to be friends with this man. 'Most people call me Merry,' she invited.

'And most people—those that don't think of me as a middle-aged cynic, that is,' he mocked, 'call me Gideon. I'm sure you have a beter idea than me what the others call me?'

'Yes—I mean, no. Er—no,' she blushed.

'Sure?' he derided.

No, she wasn't sure! She could think of a hundred names she could call him right at this minute, and she wouldn't need to repeat herself once! 'No,' she lied.

Gideon's mouth quirked as if he knew of the lie. 'We

got off to a bad start,' he said quietly. 'And as we're somehow related through the marriage of our parents I think we should make an effort to get on together.' He was completely serious now. 'Especially if it turns out you do want to get to know Anthea as your mother. Being my girl-friend is a safety valve, for both of you. You know that, don't you?'

'I don't see how,' she frowned.

'If you decide you can't accept Anthea knowing you're her daughter, really feel you can't love her, then our romance will just end, with Anthea none the wiser as to your identity.'

She could see that, but she still frowned. 'You said I look like—like her,' she reminded him. 'What if she makes the connection straight away?'

'She won't,' Gideon assured her confidently. 'Once you were out of that disgusting make-up I looked for a likeness to Anthea. I found it only because I was looking for it. If you're my girl-friend Anthea wouldn't even think of the possibility of your being her daughter. She's given up hope of ever finding you,' he added huskily.

Merry swallowed hard, feeling Anthea Steele's despair in Gideon's concern. 'Did she look for me?'

'Once you were sixteen, yes,' he nodded. 'And while a child can trace his or her parent, the parent doesn't really have the same privilege. She gave up her child, the child was happily adopted. And unless you made a claim to meet your real mother then Anthea's longing to know you would remain unanswered. I'm afraid my own investigations weren't made as fairly as Anthea's,' he told her drily.

No, she could imagine Gideon would have little patience with the rules and regulations in life, would ...em aside if they got in his way—as he had when ...er.

'I could hardly make that claim,' she murmured. 'Not when I had no idea I was adopted.'

'Have you spoken to your father since last night?'

'Yes.' She could easily recall the emotional telephone conversation she had had with her father early this morning while waiting for Gideon to arrive, her father's deep pride in her decision to meet Anthea Steele giving her a pride in herself—and in her father's unselfish love for her.

'Any problems?' Gideon was watching her intently.

'Of course not,' she told him briskly. 'My father has encouraged me from the first to meet your stepmother.'

'Much to your surprise,' he mocked.

'Not really,' she replied thoughtfully. 'My father is a very generous man.' She looked down at her hands. 'I— Do you know anything about my real father?' Colour slowly entered her cheeks.

As if understanding her reluctant curiosity Gideon's hand moved to clasp hers. 'It's all right, Merry,' he said softly. 'There's no shame in wanting to know about him. But I'm afraid the answer is no,' he straightened in his seat as they approached the airport, both hands on the steering-wheel now. 'My father knows, Anthea insisted on telling him, but I felt that part of her past was too private for me to know. Maybe one day you could ask her.'

Maybe one day, if they ever became that close. She was twenty now, and she somehow couldn't see herself accepting a new mother at this late stage in her life, especially when she had loved her adoptive mother so much.

But for the moment she felt her nervousness towards the small jet that was to transport them to Athens. She had only ever flown twice before, and each time it had been on a chartered flight, nothing like this executive jet Gideon had every intention of piloting himself. It was the latter that made her most nervous, and she sat alone in the lounge of the twelve-seater jet, her hands tightly gripping the seat as the engine roared in preparation of take-off. Gideon had callously left her here ten minutes earlier, and was even now intending to wing them up into the skies. She felt sick at the thought of it.

'All right?'

She looked up with a start, not having noticed Gideon's approach, finding him looking down at her with open amusement.

'You don't get air-sick, do you?' he mocked her intensity.

'No!' she snapped, hoping that would still be true when she got off.

'Good,' he shrugged. 'I just thought I would let you know we're about to take off.'

'Well, do it, then!'

His mouth quirked. 'I'll see you in about three hours.'

Three hours! Out here all on her own? But not by the flicker of an eyelid did she let Gideon know that bothered her. She wouldn't give him that satisfaction.

He gave another shrug, then turned and went back to join his co-pilot in the cockpit. Damn him, Merry fumed. Damn him, damn him! How was she supposed to act as if she were attracted to him when all they did was snap and snarl at each other? Act—that was the appropriate word. And she was supposed to be an actress, wasn't she? Now was the time to prove to Gideon Steele just how good an actress she was!

He came out to see her once during the flight, leaving the control of the plane in the capable hands of his co-pilot, a middle-aged man he had introduced to her earlier as Jim Sands. Merry was sweetly polite, much to his surprise, she felt sure. He left her again after only a few minutes, a wariness in the mocking blue eyes that had not been there earlier. Good, he would do well to be wary of her. She didn't intend to be cowed by his maturity and experience any longer.

She gazed out of the window as they approached Athens airport, looking down on the Parthenon, the Greek temple that the whole world knew of, standing dominantly over the city of Athens on the Acropolis, strangely beautiful against the background of modern Athens, the whole city seeming to be made up of two and three-storey blocks of flats and shops. As the plane taxied across the runway to the terminal building Merry could see the dusty, dry terrain, the dried grass swaying in the gentle breeze, the sun hot on her bare arms as she stepped down on to the ground at Gideon's side.

He held her firmly beside him as they entered the marble-floored terminal building, the formalities being quickly dealt with as Gideon's authority was clearly recognised. Jim Sands would be returning to England as soon as the jet had been refuelled.

'We'll get a taxi to Piraeus,' Gideon told her absently as the driver stowed their luggage in the boot of the car—Merry's battered red suitcase and Gideon's black leather one with a well-known brand label on the handle.

Merry was finding the sun very humid, not being a sun-worshipper herself, although Gideon seemed to revel in it; his body was already deeply tanned, not even perspiring in the black sweat-shirt, while her clothes already felt as if they were sticking to her. 'Piraeus?' she repeated irritably, climbing into the back of the taxi to sit beside him.

'That's the name of the port,' he supplied uninterestedly.

'Oh.' She lapsed into silence, feeling stupid.

It was early afternoon as they drove through the streets of Athens to the adjoining port of Piraeus, and most of the shops seemed to be closed, shutters pulled over windows to shut out the heat of the hot sun, reminding Merry that the siesta was still practised here. She couldn't blame them, she could do with a sleep herself! The last few days had been very traumatic, not allowing an easy mind for sleep at all. And soon, very soon, she was to meet her mother. She felt sick with nervousness.

'Just relax,' Gideon encouraged softly. 'I'm sure you'll love Anthea.'

Her eyes were dark with her uncertainty. 'But will she love me?'

His mouth quirked. 'As my girl-friend, probably not. But when—if she knows the truth, then yes, she'll love you.'

Merry was frowning. 'Why won't she like me as your girl-friend?' she asked suspiciously.

'I didn't say she would *dislike* you, only that she wouldn't love you,' he smiled, that devastating smile that was turning out to have such an effect on her equilibrium. 'For some reason Anthea seems to feel that none of my girl-friends are good enough for me.'

'Perhaps they aren't.'

His mouth tightened at her deliberate insult. 'I think her concern is just the usual maternal one.'

'How can her feelings towards you be maternal when she's only four years older than you are?' she scorned.

His eyes narrowed. 'Meaning?'

She couldn't meet his gaze. 'Meaning she's only four years older than you,' she repeated stubbornly, a deep flush to her cheeks as she refused to back down under his dawning anger.

'Yes,' he bit out. 'And she's been my mother for the last twelve years.'

Merry turned away from the challenge in his eyes, knowing she couldn't meet it any further. She had been curious about his relationship with her mother, but it seemed she would learn nothing from Gideon. But no man could regard a woman so near his own age as a mother-figure. Her mother was young enough to have been *his* wife.

There were many cruise ships docked in Piraeus harbour, and Merry felt the excited thrill of wondering which one they would be on. They all looked so beautiful!

Gideon paid off the driver, a deep smile of recognition grooving his face as a short, dark-haired, obviously Greek man came towards them. 'Niko!' The two men hugged a greeting, slapping each other on the back.

Merry stood to one side watching them, comparing the two men, Gideon's lean strength, the older man's portly good looks. There seemed to be many young Greeks at the harbour, and yet Gideon stood out amongst them as the most distinguished, his dress and appearance no different from theirs, but an aura of distinction about him nonetheless.

Gideon had been talking to the other man in what Merry presumed to be fluent Greek—she doubted Gideon would ever do anything by half-measures! The thought of that brought a deep flush to her cheeks. What on earth was she thinking of!

She became aware for the first time that the two men were actually talking about her now, something flattering by the way Niko's warm brown gaze caressed her slenderness.

'*Ne*,' Gideon laughed as Niko turned back to make a personal comment about her.

Merry frowned. 'What did he say?'

'I say you are beautiful young lady, and Gideon, he agree,' Niko answered for himself, his English very accented, but understandable nonetheless.

Merry smiled her relief. 'Thank you,' she blushed at the compliment.

'In Greek you would say *efharisto*,' he supplied with a grin.

'*Efharisto*,' she repeated shyly.

'Very good,' Niko laughed his enjoyment.

Gideon's mouth twisted. 'Merry is more familiar with the word *ohi*,' he drawled.

'Then perhaps you should learn to say *parakalo* more often, my friend,' Niko laughed again, slapping the younger man on the back, then he picked up their cases to move ahead of them, still grinning.

Merry walked at Gideon's side. 'What did he say? What did *you* say?' She had the feeling that whatever it was he had been mocking her.

'I told him you're more familiar with the word no,' Gideon taunted softly. 'He told me I should say please more often.'

Angry colour darkened her cheeks at the implied intimacy of such a conversation.

Gideon sighed as he saw the angry sparkle in her eyes. 'You're supposed to be my girl-friend, remember?'

She pulled her arm out of his grasp. 'Girl-friend, not *woman*!'

He shrugged. 'With me it's the same thing. I haven't had a platonic relationship with one of my women for years.'

'I can believe that!' she snapped. 'Well, this one is certainly going to be,' she warned him.

'I have no doubt about that,' he said grimly. 'But the least I can expect now is your co-operation. Well,' he said with a sudden change of mood, 'what do you think of it?'

'It' was a beautifully sleek yacht, impossible for Merry to even guess at its footage when she was actually standing on its deck. But it was a beautiful yacht, a pure glistening white, the crew moving quietly and efficiently about the deck also wearing pristine white uniforms, several of them greeting Gideon with the same familiarity as Niko had minutes earlier.

Merry looked up at the dark man at her side with bewildered eyes. 'But——'

His mouth twisted. 'Not what you were expecting, is it?' he mused.

'You know it isn't!' She was getting a little tired of being the brunt of his amusement. 'I thought it would be one of the cruise ships. You knew I did,' she accused.

'Yes,' he nodded, leading the way down some stairs to the cabins. 'But this is so much more comfortable.'

She could see that, had had a brief glimpse of luxurious lounges, the cabin Gideon now showed her into being more suited to one of London's leading hotels than a ship. The carpet was thick and deep, its cream colour a startling contrast to the brown quilt on the bed, cream scatter cushions lying casually on top of this, while the wall behind the bed was completely covered in mirrors, giving the room an even bigger appearance than it really was. A vase of fresh roses stood on the dressing-table, also some books and magazines. The cabin was big and beautiful, and totally unbelievable when she had been expecting a minute cabin in the bowels of a cruise ship.

'Cheer up,' Gideon misunderstood her bewilderment. 'Maybe I'll take you on a cruise next time.'

'*You* will?' Her eyes widened.

'Why not—little sister?' he drawled mockingly, his arms folded across his broad chest.

'I'm not your sister,' she snapped, seeing her suitcase had already been placed beside the bed, probably by Niko, although the other man seemed to have disappeared now.

'No, you aren't,' Gideon pulled her sharply against him, angry himself now, 'but you are supposed to be my girl-friend. And my girl-friends don't usually walk around scowling at everyone.'

Merry pushed against his chest, not liking being this close to him. He was too damned overpowering for her peace of mind. 'You keep them happier than that, I suppose?' she scorned, her expression defiant.

'Exactly,' he bit out. 'So try and look more as if you enjoy my touch. Maybe I should try to make you like my kisses too.'

She could see the intent in his face, and all the rebellion went out of her as she began to tremble. 'No——'

'Yes,' he insisted grimly. 'You've been nothing but bad-tempered and disagreeable ever since we left England, and I don't intend to put up with it any longer.'

She gave an angry gasp. '*You* don't——'

'Oh, shut up, you little hellion,' he dismissed her protest wearily. 'Just shut up.' His head bent and he kissed her hard on the mouth.

Merry had been in the middle of protesting at this further rudeness at the time, a mistake on her part as he deepened the kiss, moving his lips erotically against hers until the fight went out of her, until her hands longed to be free of his constricting arms to move up to his nape and caress the dark hair there. He held her against the hardness of his body, his hands moving over her back in slow exploration. As she made no murmur of protest he moved further, searching the moist sweetness of her mouth, evoking a warm pleasure through her body that made her legs tremble.

'Oh! I—I'll come back later. I—Sorry!' The door to the cabin closed with a slam.

Merry instantly wrenched away from Gideon, breathing heavily, hardly able to believe that mocking mouth could have such a devastating effect on her. Especially as he seemed unmoved by the encounter himself; the deep blue eyes were challenging.

She turned away. 'Who was that?'

'Probably one of the cabin staff come to unpack for you,' he dismissed.

She swallowed hard. 'Don't you care——? She saw——'

'A lot of people will "see" before the end of the two weeks,' Gideon mocked. 'I intend kissing my girl-friend a lot during this holiday.'

'You will not——'

'I will, Meredith,' he told her in a tone that brooked no further argument. 'And you'll damn well enjoy it! That shouldn't be too difficult,' he taunted.

She blushed at his knowledge of how easily she had succumbed to his experienced caresses. 'I don't want you to kiss me again,' she snapped.

'Why? Do you have a boy-friend who'll object?' He looked as if the idea had just occurred to him.

'*I* object,' she told him pointedly. 'Very much, as it happens.'

Gideon began to look bored by the subject, as if her opinion weren't of much importance, especially to him. 'You came here knowing under what circumstances you would be introduced to everyone. Use that talent you seem to think you have.'

She drew in an angry breath at the insult. 'Oh, I have it, Gideon,' she rasped. 'You'll see how much.'

'I'll look forward to it,' he mocked. 'Now do whatever it is you women do when you "freshen up", and I'll meet you on deck in half an hour.'

She eyed him suspiciously. 'Where are we going?'

His mouth twisted. 'I'd be failing in my duty as your boy-friend if I didn't take you to see the Parthenon. You can't come to Athens and not go there. And by the time we get back maybe the others will have returned,' the last he added almost to himself.

'Where are they?' she frowned, having noticed they seemed to be the only visible guests on board, the only other people she had seen appearing to be the crew—and there were a lot of them. This was definitely a luxury yacht in the fullest sense of the word.

'Glyfada,' Gideon supplied. 'Visiting a friend's villa there, according to Niko. I'm glad we arrived too late to join them.'

'Why?' she frowned, wondering if he could possibly be nervous about her first meeting with Anthea too.

'Astra tends to—monopolise,' he grimaced.

Her mouth twisted as she realised his reasons were entirely selfish. 'In other words, she's attracted to you and you don't reciprocate.'

His stance was relaxed, his fingers splayed out across his thigh as his hand rested there. 'I did, once. And only once,' he added derisively.

'That's disgusting!' Merry gasped.

'It wasn't at the time. But that was ten years ago. Unfortunately, Astra never gives up.'

'Poor Astra,' she mumbled, swinging her case up on the bed to get out her fresh clothing. She was feeling hot and sticky after the flight and taxi drive here.

'Don't be long,' Gideon warned. 'I'll be next door if you should happen to get lost.'

She knew that was a possibility; she had found the intricacies of the winding corridors very confusing on her way down here. If they had been on a full sized cruise ship she would probably have spent the whole of the two weeks in a state of confusion!

She knew that she had indeed got lost when she found herself in the galley of the yacht instead of up on deck. Fortunately Niko came to her rescue, turning out to be one of the cooks, and he took her up on deck himself.

'I return your beautiful lady—reluctantly,' Niko told

Gideon as he slowly raised himself from the lounger he had been stretched out on, looking as if he had been there some time.

He had changed too, and was now wearing tight denims and a fitted blue shirt with short sleeves, showing the muscled strength of his arms. 'Thanks, Niko,' he grimaced at the other man, putting his arm about Merry's waist and holding her there as she would have flinched from his arm making contact with her warm flesh, her lemon halter-necked top reaching just below her uptilted breasts, her black denims fitting tautly to her slender hips. Gideon gave her an appreciative look. 'I'll keep a better eye on her in future.'

'I should,' the other man nodded, 'or someone will steal her from you.'

'Not a chance,' Gideon said confidently. 'Hm, sweetheart?' he looked down at her challengingly.

She gave him a warm smile, snuggling into his side. 'Not one,' she said throatily.

His mouth quirked. 'Not bad,' he murmured for her ears alone, his head going back as he spoke to Niko. 'We'd better be going. See you later.'

'Enjoy my country,' Niko smiled.

'Are all the crew on the yacht Greek?' Merry stepped away from Gideon as they moved down on to the deck area, feeling no need to keep up the pretence when they were alone.

He shrugged. 'Some. Some English. Some American. We have no prejudices,' he taunted. 'And they all get along together just fine,' he answered her next question.

The taxi drove them through the streets of Athens. The shops were still closed, something Merry found very strange.

'Unlike England the main shops in Athens close for the day at one-thirty on a Saturday,' Gideon explained.

'They would normally still be closed at this time anyway, they don't usually re-open until at least four-thirty, sometimes later.' He quirked one dark eyebrow. 'You weren't thinking of dragging me off to the shops, were you?'

Her eyes glowed with mischief. She felt refreshed from the shower she had taken, her hair pulled back in a single plait down her spine, giving her a very youthful appearance, a fact Gideon had viewed with a jaundiced eye when she had first joined him on deck. He had wisely said nothing, possibly seeing the light of challenge in her eyes. 'That's hardly the attitude of a doting boy-friend,' she taunted.

'I'm not that doting!'

She laughed softly. 'I didn't think so. Oh, what's that?' she cried excitedly as she spotted a large arch, with the tall pillars of another building behind it, ancient Athens somehow all mixed up with the confusion of the new.

'The Arch of Hadrian,' Gideon supplied knowledgeably. 'It's the mark of the division between the old part of the city built by the Greeks, and the Roman extension by Hadrian.'

'It's beautiful,' she turned to look at it. 'The same Hadrian who built the wall in England?'

'The same,' he nodded.

As they drove towards the Acropolis Merry had a chance to see the mountains in the hazy distance; the sun was very hot. 'I had no idea Athens was surrounded by mountains.' She was awe-struck.

'Athens stands in a basin, the Aegean on one side, the mountains surrounding the others.' Once again Gideon showed his knowledge of the city.

The taxi pulled into the roadside at the foot of the enormous rock. Several coaches were already parked there, and Gideon paid the driver as Merry unclipped her camera to take photographs.

'It's better from the top.' Gideon clasped her elbow as they began to walk up the stone pathway. Merry was visibly breathing hard by the time they reached the top. 'You're out of condition,' Gideon mocked as he paid over the drachma for them to go to see the ancient ruins.

It was all so vast and beautiful, impossible to take in, although Merry did her best, taking dozens of photographs of the Parthenon and other ruins, finding when they reached the top that it wasn't the only temple on the Acropolis but one of many, although certainly the biggest.

'Stand there.' Gideon took her camera from her, stepping back to take a photograph of her in front of the Parthenon. 'Let me have a copy of that when you get them developed,' he drawled.

'Why?' she asked suspiciously.

'The Parthenon is a temple of Athena, the Virgin. I have a feeling that having you stand in front of such a temple is very apt.'

She turned away from his derision. 'I suppose a trite remark like that can be expected from a *cynic* like you,' she said coldly. 'You're only standing amongst beauty that has survived for almost two and a half *thousand* years!' Seeing this beautiful architecture that had survived since before Christ had given her a sense of her own insignificance. She felt sure it did that to everyone who came here.

Or *almost* everyone, she thought, shooting Gideon a resentful glance as he appeared completely bored by the whole thing. Well, she wasn't ashamed to play tourist, after all, that was what she was. And she doubted she would ever get the chance to come back to these places again.

'Beautiful!' Gideon sighed as they drove back to the yacht.

Merry gave him a sharp look. 'Beautiful ...?' She was too overawed by the majesty of the Acropolis for his mockery at this moment.

'Yes,' he smiled at her suspicion. 'To think that thousands of years ago it took thousands of men nine years just to build the Parthenon.' He gave a rueful grimace. 'Nowadays you're lucky if a building stays *up* nine years!'

His levity broke her own mood of resentment as she returned his smile. A sudden wave of nervousness washed over her, something she had been fighting all day. 'Oh, Gideon, will she like me?' She clutched at his hand, not caring if he saw her weakness, wanting only his comfort in this world of wealth and cynicism she suddenly seemed to have been thrust into.

'She will.' He didn't mock her uncertainty, merely continued to hold her hand in his strong capable one, and he was still holding it as they returned on board the yacht.

'Gideon!'

Merry froze as a woman launched herself into Gideon's arms, her hand at last released as he moved to steady her. As he held her at arm's length Merry could at least see it wasn't her mother; this woman was tall, leggy and blonde, probably in her early thirties. Just the right age for Gideon, according to him. Was this one of his women?

'Darling!' the woman glowed up at him. She was very beautiful, although her make-up was heavier than Merry liked for herself.

But Gideon showed no such inhibitions, and returned the woman's kiss of greeting. 'Linda,' he said huskily. 'How good to see you again! I——'

'If you'll excuse me, darling,' Merry interrupted softly, sure that she had been completely forgotten by Gideon in that moment. So much for *her* acting! 'I think I'll go and change before dinner.'

Shrewd brown eyes were turned on her, as the woman called Linda seemed to notice her for the first time, her gaze completely critical as she seemed to price every article of clothing Merry wore, from the halter top down to the rope sandals. The whole lot hadn't cost fifty pounds!

Gideon smoothly effected the introductions. 'Can you find your way back to the cabin?' he asked Merry.

'*The* cabin?' Linda Martin drawled. 'Really, Gideon, you surely aren't flaunting this child as your mistress in front of Anthea and Samuel?'

Anger flared briefly in deep blue eyes, although Gideon's smile didn't waver. 'My cabin is next to Meredith's,' he drawled. 'Although don't be fooled by this youthful exterior,' he flicked Merry's plait. 'Merry is far from being a child.'

She flushed at his implication, but the light of challenge shone in her eyes as she put her arm through the crook of his, reaching up on tiptoe to kiss him on the cheek, refusing to kiss his mouth where the other woman's lip-gloss was in evidence. 'I had a good teacher,' she said throatily. 'I'll see you later, darling. So nice to have met you, Miss Martin. No doubt I'll see you again later too.'

'No doubt,' the other woman drawled uninterestedly, and turned away. 'I have so much to talk to you about, Gideon.' She led him away.

Merry watched as Gideon's dark head bent close to the blonde one as he listened to the other woman's throaty chatter. Thank goodness she wasn't really his girl-friend, she would have been totally demoralised by Linda Martin's possessive air where he was concerned. And like the flirt that he was, Gideon was lapping it up.

Not that that bothered Merry for the moment; right now she was more interested in what she should wear to meet her mother for the first time.

She had brought several evening dresses with her, plus a couple of long skirts with interchangeable tops. And now she was glad she had, sure that the women on board, if they were all like Linda Martin, would be dressing for dinner, as the men would be putting on evening suits. No doubt Gideon would look magnificent in a dinner suit, having the height and body for it.

Well, he wouldn't be ashamed of her appearance either, she would make sure of that. But she was also very conscious of wanting Anthea Steele to approve of her appearance. After all, it could be difficult to make the right impression when you were meeting your mother for the first time in twenty years.

She chose her white gown, strapless, fitting over her uptilted breasts and waist before flowing to the floor, the daring neckline alleviated by the chiffon jacket that dulled her creamy flesh to a mere shadow. Her hair she brushed until it gleamed, securing it skilfully on top of her head, leaving her neck strangely vulnerable and putting into prominence her high cheekbones. The more sophisticated style also had the effect of adding maturity, and when Gideon knocked on her cabin door at seven-thirty she greeted him with confidence.

She had been right about him looking magnificent in evening clothes; the white dinner jacket fitted tautly across his shoulders, the snowy white shirt having a frill-front, his bow-tie black velvet, the black fitted evening trousers emphasising the lean length of his legs.

But if she was fascinated by his appearance he was equally bemused by hers, making no effort to hide his surprise.

'So the child can be a woman,' he mused, his eyes a warm blue. 'In that case I'm glad I bought you these.'

'These...?' Merry blinked her puzzlement as he brought out a black, square jewellery box. 'Oh no!' Her eyes widened in horror as he opened it to reveal a necklace and matching droplet earrings in the same diamond and gold design. 'No!' she repeated firmly as she took in the full implications of wearing such jewellery. She would look like no more than a bought-and-paid-for mistress!

Gideon stopped in the process of taking the necklace from its velvet nest, frowning at her. 'No?'

'That's what I said!' Her mouth was tight.

'Every other woman in that room is going to be dripping in jewels,' he ground out. 'All trying to outdo the other.'

Her confidence wavered for a moment. 'How many other women?'

'A dozen or so.'

That meant there must be at least a dozen men as well. She hadn't realised there would be so many people on board. 'Then I'll stand out as the only woman *not* wearing jewellery, won't I?' she said firmly.

'Meredith——'

'Gideon!' Green eyes met his unwaveringly.

He gave an impatient sigh and snapped shut the jewellery case. 'Are you always this damned stubborn?'

She smiled mischievously. 'Always. Now, tell me where we go after Athens?'

'Bored with it already?' He accepted her change of subject, opening the door for them to leave.

'No, just curious.' She picked the jewellery case up from the dressing-table and handed it to him. 'You forgot this,' she arched one dark brow at him.

He took the case, unlocking the cabin next door to throw the jewellery box on the bed. 'We go to Turkey next,' he told her as he relocked the door.

Merry had had a brief glimpse of a cabin similar to her own, except that Gideon seemed to have discarded his clothes all over the room. 'You're untidy,' she told him as they went up to the dining-room.

'A man's allowed one vice.' His hand was firm on her elbow.

'One?' she taunted.

'Women aren't a vice, Merry,' he drawled softly as they approached the noise of people talking in the dining-room. 'To some men they're a necessity.'

'You?'

'Yes, me,' he admitted unashamedly.

'Then at least those people in there will know what attracted me to you *other* than the jewellery I won't wear,' she quirked a mocking brow at him.

His mouth twitched with humour, then he smiled, and finally he laughed softly. 'You amuse me, if nothing else, little sister.'

Her eyes flashed at the title, then her head went back as they entered the dining-room, the subdued lighting adding elegance and charm to the long dining-table, the silver cutlery gleaming brightly, the wine glasses pure crystal, the perfume of the roses in the central decoration heady and sweet.

People stood about the room in clusters of threes and fours, chatting in loud voices most of them already deeply tanned from the weeks they had already spent in the Mediterranean. As Gideon had said, all the women were dripping in jewels, their dresses beautiful and shimmering, the men all wearing dinner suits or cocktail jackets. The elegant rich, Merry decided ruefully.

Gideon gently squeezed her arm. 'Anthea,' he told her softly.

He needn't have bothered, she had already guessed which one of the beautiful women was her mother. Like her, Anthea Steele was small and slender, her black hair worn to her shoulders in soft curls, her face still breathtakingly beautiful. And, as if becoming aware of their presence, the other woman turned in their direction, Merry finding herself looking into eyes as green as her own.

CHAPTER FOUR

IT was strange to look at the woman she knew to be her mother, knowing that she paled slightly, seeing the older woman's gaze become troubled for a moment before her attention was distracted by the man at her side. Merry's gaze shifted to the man; his similarity to Gideon was too strong for him to be anyone but Samuel Steele, Gideon's father, although where Gideon's hair was so dark the older man's was iron-grey.

Gideon held her easily at his side as the other couple came towards them. 'That's us in twenty years' time,' he murmured, as shaken by the realisation as she was. 'What we'll look like.'

She didn't have time for a reply, but stood back as Anthea greeted him with obvious warmth, his father shaking his hand.

'This is Meredith.' He pulled her forward, his arm about her waist. 'Meredith Charles,' he repeated, looking at the other couple to see if there was any reaction to his announcement. There wasn't.

'Glad to meet you, my dear.' Samuel Steele shook her hand.

'She's charming, Gideon,' Anthea told him huskily as she kissed Merry warmly on the cheek. 'I'm so sorry we weren't here to meet you when you arrived,' she smiled. 'But Gideon was very vague about what time you would be getting here.'

Merry felt tongue-tied, wondering why no one else but Gideon and herself could see her likeness to Anthea. To her it was blazingly obvious, even the husky tone of her voice was similar to the other woman's. But no one else did seem aware of it, and she breathed easier.

Gideon smiled confidently. 'I wanted Meredith to myself this afternoon.'

'I can see why,' his father teased lightly. 'I hope you'll enjoy your holiday with us, Meredith.'

'Merry,' she corrected softly. 'Most people call me Merry. Gideon just enjoys being—contrary at times.'

Samuel Steele's eyes had narrowed at the first sound of her voice, although he laughed at the latter. 'I've noticed that about my son too.'

'Don't encourage her, Dad,' Gideon said dryly. 'She manages quite well on her own!'

All four of them laughed, and Merry couldn't help but admire her mother's beauty. Although she noticed the older woman's gaiety seemed forced at times as they ate their meal, a fact Samuel Steele was quick to notice; his anxious gaze was often on his wife. Anthea gave him loving smiles if she encountered those gazes, clear reassuring smiles that spoke of their true affection for each other. Their obvious love for each other made Merry ashamed of the accusation she had once made to Gideon about Anthea marrying the older man for his money.

But she had no chance to talk to Gideon about her mistake, because his attention was monopolised by Linda Martin, who sat on his other side. The blonde woman had acknowledged her presence with an abrupt nod of her head before directing her conversation exclusively at Gideon, something he didn't seem averse to in the least.

'Don't mind Linda,' the man sitting to her left said softly. 'She and Gideon are old friends.'

She turned to smile at the man, remembering that Gideon had introduced him as Michael Woods. 'I don't mind,' she dismissed. 'Gideon and I are new friends,' she said pointedly.

Michael laughed appreciatively. He was a man of Gideon's age, with over-long fair hair and friendly blue eyes, a good-looking man in a relaxed easygoing way, with none of the aura of danger that surrounded Gideon. 'I believe Linda may have finally met her match,' he chuckled. 'In fact, I believe all the women here, with the exception of Anthea, have met their match.'

Merry looked taken aback. '*All* of them?'

'Most of them,' he amended easily. 'But, like Linda, they gave up in the end and married someone else. Second best maybe, but good marriages nonetheless.'

She didn't miss the trace of bitterness in his voice and expression, wondering which one of these bejewelled women was his wife. 'I didn't realise Linda was married,' she reassessed the situation.

'She isn't,' Michael said hardly, taking a large swallow of his wine. 'Our wedding takes place next month.'

Compassion filled her eyes. 'I didn't know——'

'Why should you?' he smiled again, dispelling his mood of gloom. 'A doctor is pretty dull stuff compared to a film director, you know,' he teased her with his eyes.

'Really?' she returned dryly. 'When you're an actress that isn't always so.'

'An actress, hm?' he sat back in his chair, the rest of the people at the table ceasing to exist as they talked softly. 'And which of Gideon's films have you appeared in? You'll have to excuse my ignorance, I rarely have the time to go to the cinema.'

Merry had stiffened at the derision in his question, guessing that he spoke out of jealousy. Linda's husky laugh of pleasure was clearly discernible to them both, although it made Michael's words no less hurtful to her. 'Only Mediterranean cruises, it seems.' She looked at him steadily.

Dull colour flushed his cheeks. 'Hell, I'm sorry,' he sighed. 'I shouldn't take my jealousy out on you. I just didn't expect to see Gideon again until after I had my wedding ring on Linda's finger. But that was no excuse to snap at you.'

She could sympathise with him; she had had no idea from Linda's behaviour that she was engaged to be married. It certainly didn't seem to inhibit her. 'I haven't appeared in any of Gideon's films,' she answered him. 'And I'm not going to,' she answered his next question before he asked it. 'Gideon doesn't think I'm talented enough.'

Blue eyes widened in disbelief. 'He doesn't?'

'No,' she laughed at his incredulity, not noticing the puzzled attention of Samuel Steele resting on her briefly, a question in the blue eyes so like his son's, before his attention was diverted by the woman sitting at his side. Merry continued to smile. 'Although I'm hoping to prove him wrong about that.'

Michael sobered. 'Merry——'

'Not in that way,' she snapped. 'Gideon and I are friends, and it isn't the sort of friendship that—trades on the relationship.'

'My dear, I'm sorry if I——'

'Merry, would you like to take a walk on deck?'

She turned with a start at the sound of Gideon's rough voice, his steely gaze fixed on Michael Woods' hand as it clasped hers in his regret. She slowly extracted her hand under the intensity of that stare and stood up next to Gideon. 'I'd love to.' She kept her eyes downcast. 'Excuse me, Michael.'

Gideon's fingers were painful on her arm as he all but dragged her out on deck. 'A good start, Merry,' he bit out. 'You all but threw yourself at the man!'

Anger blazed at his accusation. 'While you flirted with his fiancée!'

His jaw was rigid. 'A fact I've just been acquainted with.'

'Oh yes?' her sarcasm taunted.

He flushed. 'I've been in the States for some time. I had no idea ...'

Merry could almost have laughed at his bad humour. This man liked to flirt, enjoyed it, but it appeared not with a woman who belonged to another man. Suddenly her thoughts of him and Anthea seemed as wrong as the ones she had had about Anthea marrying his father for his money. 'Tell me how my—how Anthea met your father?' she prompted huskily.

Gideon leant on the handrail, looking over at the lights that were the city of Athens. 'She became his secretary—oh, it must be about fifteen years ago now. My mother had already been dead for six years, and while my father had loved her very much, he was ready to love again. I was nineteen when he met Anthea, and I knew straight away that he loved her, could see the life flowing back into him,' he spoke softly, his thoughts inwards, Merry almost forgotten. 'But she fought against admitting her feelings for him,' Gideon smiled at the memory. 'God, how she fought! But my father can be a very determined man——'

'Like you,' she mocked, touched by the story he was telling her.

'Like me,' he turned to smile at her. 'It took my father three years to wear her down, to get her to marry him. They've been happy together, I'm sure of it.'

'So am I,' she touched his arm. 'Gideon, I'm so sorry for what I said before. I didn't know——'

'Of course you didn't.' He took her hand in his as the other guests joined them on deck. 'We're leaving for Turkey now,' he told her.

They stood on deck and watched the lights of Athens until they left the port of Piraeus and passed out into the Aegean Sea. There could surely be nothing more romantic than standing beneath the stars on a luxury yacht, the beauty of Greece behind them the mysteries of Turkey in front of them.

And yet in that moment Merry couldn't appreciate it; the strange feelings of the yacht moving beneath her was doing strange things to her stomach. She had never sailed before, only ever been in a rowing-boat on a lake, and she didn't think that really counted. Being on the yacht when it was moving gave her a strange sinking sensation in her lower stomach, unlike anything she had ever experienced before, and she wished she hadn't drunk the wine with her dinner.

The yacht was a blaze of lights that reflected on the blue water beneath them as they cut smoothly through the waves, and several of the party strolled about in the warm air, while others sat on the outside lounge area drinking and talking.

'Shall we join them?' Gideon suggested.

Merry wasn't sure she felt like it, but she could hardly go to her cabin at ten o'clock at night—especially as it was only seven o'clock in England! She hadn't thought of the time difference since Gideon had instructed her to put her watch forward three hours when they were on the plane.

For all that it must have been a tiring day for Gideon, the drive to Gatwick, the piloting of the flight to Athens, and an afternoon up the Acropolis, Gideon looked as fresh as he had first thing this morning.

And she was beginning to feel decidedly the worse for wear, although the surging motion of the yacht didn't feel quite as bad once she was sitting down, Gideon relaxed in the chair at her side.

He spoke softly to his father and Anthea, and once

again Merry looked shyly at the woman who was her mother. She was a stranger to her, someone she had barely spoken half a dozen words to, and yet she could feel the tie between them.

As if sensing her regard Anthea turned to smile at her, her green eyes warm and friendly, her smile natural. 'Gideon tells us you're an actress,' she prompted.

Merry slanted him a mocking glance. 'Did he?'

'Yes, darling, I did,' he stated firmly, taking her hand in his, the fingers bruising as they laced through hers.

'Gideon doesn't like actresses,' she confided in the other woman, enjoying being able to taunt him in this way when he couldn't hit back.

'That isn't so,' his mouth smiled, but his eyes remained hard. 'Some of my best friends are actresses.'

'And you told me you didn't make friends of women,' she mocked.

'I'm your—friend, aren't I?' he ground out, his fingers tightening painfully now.

She eyed him thoughtfully, seeing his tension rising to snapping point, then very wisely quit while she was still ahead. 'Yes, of course,' she laughed lightly.

Samuel Steele was watching them with amusement, although his main attention seemed to be on Meredith, as if something about her puzzled him. Merry became aware of his frowning gaze, realising that he was as astute as his son, possibly more so. It would never do to arouse his suspicions, not until she was completely sure she could accept Anthea's relationship to her.

'I'm only teasing, darling,' she laughed, and bent over to kiss Gideon on the mouth, sensing his surprise before his mouth opened and he kissed her back. She pulled away from him the moment she sensed his response, seeing the glitter of anger in his eyes before she turned to Anthea. 'Gideon hates to be teased,' she confided.

'I know,' the other woman laughed too.

'He always did.' Samuel joined in the mockery of his son, not in the least concerned by Gideon's glowering expression.

'Well, he's been "teased" enough for one night.' Gideon stood up, pulling Merry to her feet too. 'I intend taking this young lady away to a dark place and making love to her.'

She felt the hot colour flooding her cheeks, barely aware of his father's chiding comment. Gideon merely laughed, and swung her away from the chattering people, leading her towards the darkened area of the bow deck.

His humour faded as soon as they were safely away from the lighted area, and he swung her round roughly in the darkness. 'You play with fire and you're going to get hurt, little girl!' he ground out, his mouth coming down forcefully on hers as he bent her to his will, pushing her into the black darkness of a doorway.

'No, Gideon!' She pushed against him as he buried his face in her throat. 'Gideon, stop this!' she pleaded as he refused to relent in his assault on her.

He raised his head. 'Isn't this what all young girls crave, to be made love to in the moonlight?' he derided harshly.

'Not this young girl.' She pulled out of his arms, glaring at him as she smoothed her dress. 'But that isn't what's important at the moment——'

'I think it is,' he drawled. 'You wouldn't have been trying to anger me into making this relationship a real one, would you?'

She drew in an angry breath. 'You conceited idiot! How dare you——'

'All right, all right,' he chuckled at her fury, his anger fading. 'But you're beautiful when you're angry. The first time I met you those green eyes flashed a warning at me, and they've been doing it ever since.'

She was too angry to listen to him. 'I wouldn't want to go to bed with you if you were the last man on earth!'

His mouth tightened. 'Not very original, but effective nonetheless. And the feeling is mutual. Now what's so important to you?' he returned to her earlier statement.

Merry chewed on her bottom lip, then moved to the railing, seeing the white spray of the sea coming off the bow of the yacht. She turned away quickly, swallowing hard, that uneasy feeling returning to her stomach. 'I think your father suspects something.'

'What do you mean by that?' he frowned.

She shrugged. 'He keeps looking at me.'

Gideon grimaced. 'That isn't so surprising, you're acting like an idiot. First of all you flirt with Michael, then you start sniping at me. My father probably thinks we've argued.'

She knew he was right in his criticism, but being his girl-friend was probably the hardest role she had ever had to play. The relationship didn't end after two or three hours when you stepped off the stage, it just went on and on, would continue for a further two weeks.

'You didn't help by flirting with Linda——' she began.

'I was talking to her——'

'Flirting!'

'Oh, for God's sake!' he turned away from her. 'Let's go back in, we aren't accomplishing anything here.'

Merry walked stiffly at his side, her awkwardness not helped by the fact that the first person they met when they went into the lounge was Linda. Merry felt really ill now, the rich food and the wine, added to the tension, was making her stomach churn. The never-ending movement of the yacht wasn't helping her queasiness.

She touched Gideon's arm. 'I'm going to my cabin,' she told him softly.

'Sulking?' he snapped.

'No,' she shook her head wearily, feeling too sick to argue.

His eyes narrowed on her pale face. 'Don't you feel well?'

'No, I——'

'You surely aren't feeling seasick?' Linda Martin's husky voice taunted. 'It's like a millpond out there!'

Merry swallowed hard, dreading to think what it would be like when it was classed as 'rough'! 'Of course I'm not feeling seasick,' she dismissed brittlely. 'I'm just tired.'

'And I thought the young had all the energy!' Once again the older woman derided her youth.

'No,' Merry answered steadily. 'We just use it more wisely. Now if you'll both excuse me ...' She had to leave before she made a fool of herself and was ill all over the deep-pile carpet in the comfortably elegant lounge.

'I'll come with you,' Gideon offered.

'No!' her voice was sharp. 'Don't let me break up your evening too—darling,' she put on as an afterthought. 'I'll see you later,' she added for the other woman's benefit.

Amusement darkened his eyes. 'I won't wake you if you're asleep,' he drawled.

Linda Martin looked angry by the intimate turn the conversation had taken, and it was her cutting barb to Gideon about cradle-snatching that enabled Meredith to reach her cabin without disgracing herself. There had been no doubting Gideon's own snapped reply. Certainly Linda hadn't found favour with him tonight.

But she didn't care about that as she staggered into the bathroom, leaving the door open, the room feeling very claustrophobic now that she was out of the sea breeze. The swaying of the floor beneath her finally proved too much, and she lost the contents of her stomach with much less dignity than she had eaten them.

She felt slightly better as she fell on to the bed, although her reflection in the mirrored wall behind her showed she had a slightly green tinge to her skin. She switched off the light with a snap, the only sound the hum of the air-conditioning.

Somewhere in the uneasy sleep she drifted off into she heard laughter and doors closing as the other guests retired to their cabins. She turned over with a groan, sure she was dying, wishing the world would stop swaying.

But it didn't, if anything it seemed to get worse as the night progressed. Merry finally woke with a start, her eyes focusing on the luminous clock on the bedside table. Three o'clock. Heavens, the night was only half over. She was going to die, she was definitely going to die!

She lay as still as she could curled into the foetal position, finding that every movement made her head spin and her stomach churn. She had to get up. She *had* to!

As soon as she had swayed to her feet she knew it was a mistake, and made a mad dash for the adjoining bathroom, once again only just making it in time. This time she sank weakly on to the floor, crying quietly, sure that she couldn't have anything left in her stomach now.

'Meredith? Good God, Merry——!' Gideon came down on his haunches beside her, smoothing her straggled hair back from her face. 'You really are seasick,' he said slowly.

Her sobs deepened, with embarrassment as much as

anything. She was in a terrible state, the white dress all stained and creased, most of her hair still secure on the top of her head, the rest of it hanging limply about her face, her make-up streaked all down her cheeks.

'It's all right, love.' Gideon pulled her up into his arms, cradling her against him.

'I need—I need to wash,' she pushed feebly against him. 'I feel dirty, and——'

'You need the doctor,' Gideon told her grimly.

'No, please,' she looked up at him with distressed eyes. 'Please, Gideon, not like this. Let me change first.'

'You need help—medical help.'

'But not like this!' She began to cry again. 'You said you were taking me on a cruise, to meet my mother, to relax in the sunshine. And instead I'm dying. Dying . . .!' she choked.

'All right, Merry,' he soothed, and sat her down on the bed.

'Where are you going?' she wailed as he moved away, not even noticing that he only wore black silk pyjama trousers, and that his chest was muscled and deeply tanned, covered in wiry dark hair.

He turned back at the bathroom door, his gaze sympathetic as it rested on her desolate figure. 'I'm going to run you a shower.'

'Oh, I don't think I can——'

'I'll help you.' He turned on the taps to the right temperature.

'No!' She recoiled at the intimacy even in her dazed state.

'You're in no condition to object, Merry,' Gideon mused, moving around her to unpin her hair, taking off the white chiffon jacket before unzipping her gown.

He was right, she was in no state to object. And she didn't, not when he slid the gown expertly down her body, unclasped her bra, and eased the tiny bikini briefs down her legs. Nor did she object when he helped her stand under the hot water, washing her hair for her, drying her gently all over with a towel as she stood naked before him.

'Better?' he asked huskily as he slipped her white cotton nightgown over her head.

Tears filled her eyes. 'You've been so kind, Gideon, I'll never forget this.'

'You will,' he said dryly. 'Probably tomorrow, if I know your temper, and I think I do. Now lie down, there's a good girl.'

'My teeth——'

'All right,' he sighed, squeezing toothpaste on to her brush for her.

'Thank you.' She turned to him gratefully, letting him help her beneath the bedcovers, feeling like the little girl he treated her as when he tucked the sheets up beneath her chin.

'Now I'm going to call Anthea's doctor——'

'Michael?' her eyes widened in panic.

'Yes,' he sighed, halting in the process of dialling the doctor's number.

'Oh no, don't! Please!' she begged.

'Why the hell not?' anger deepened his voice.

'I don't—I don't want him to see me like this.' She turned away.

'Why the hell not?' Gideon's eyes narrowed. 'You're attracted to him,' he accused.

'No! I just—I don't want Linda to know,' she admitted miserably. 'I can't help being seasick, Gideon,' she clasped his hand. 'I don't want to be riduculed for it.'

His face darkened. 'You obstinate little fool!' He pulled her roughly up off the bed, crushing her mouth with his. 'Now,' he eyes glittered warningly, 'I'm going to get Michael in here to see you. And if anyone ridicules you they'll have me to deal with. Okay?'

'Okay.' She looked up at him trustingly, completely cowed by that kiss.

His expression softened. 'So I can call Michael?'

Merry nodded, feeling too weak to argue any further, the feeling of sickness not going on its own. And she couldn't bear to feel like this any longer.

She was hardly aware of Michael Woods' presence, his soothing hands as he examined her, the injection he gave her, his softly murmured words of advice to Gideon before he quietly left them.

Gideon came to sit beside her, smoothing back her hair from her pale face. 'That wasn't so bad, now was it?'

Her lids began to feel heavy, and she had trouble focusing on him. 'You didn't have the injection in your——'

'Naughty, naughty, Merry,' he mocked, pulling back the bedclothes at her side and sitting down beside her.

Merry felt the cool air on her legs, forcing her eyes open as the injection began to work. 'What are you doing?' her words were slurred.

'Michael said I should spend the night with you, in case you need help again.' He swung into the bed beside her. 'And I have no intention of sleeping in the chair when there's a double bed here.'

'But, Gideon——'

'Go to sleep, Merry.' He pulled her head down on to his chest. 'Just think of me as a nice soft pillow,' he derided.

'But you aren't soft, you're——'

'Yes?' He looked down at her.

Merry snuggled against him in her sleep, her sigh one of deep contentment, her fingers splayed possessively across his chest, her legs entangling with his.

CHAPTER FIVE

SHE awoke with a feeling of well-being. The nausea had all but gone now, and bright sunshine was warming the room through the porthole window.

With the resilience of the young she pushed the sheet back and swung her legs to the floor, at once wishing she hadn't as feelings of weakness washed over her. She was just wondering if she could make it to the bathroom when the cabin door opened and Gideon came in, his only clothing a pair of black swimming trunks, his bare chest and legs deeply tanned.

'Good morning, Merry,' he greeted cheerfully, putting the tray he carried down on the table in the lounge area of the cabin. 'Breakfast,' he explained as he began to arrange the contents on the table.

As Merry watched him the full horror of last night came back to her, erasing what little colour there was in her cheeks. Not only had she made a complete idiot of herself by being seasick in relatively calm waters, she had also spent the night in this man's arms, knew the intimate touch of those broad shoulders, the hardness of his body, the strength of his arms.

She watched the play of muscles across his back, the flat tautness of his stomach, his powerful thighs, the long length of his legs. She had spent the night with him, the pillow beside hers on the bed still bore the imprint of his head!

'There,' he turned to face her, the blue eyes warm, 'just a light breakfast, Michael said, so I—Merry?' he frowned as he saw the way she was avoiding his gaze. 'What is it?' He came over to her, sitting beside her to lift her chin so that she had no choice but to look at him. 'Do you still feel ill?'

'I—A little,' she admitted, although she knew that her feelings of weakness at this moment weren't due to being ill. This close to Gideon she was aware of his elusive aftershave, of the utterly male smell of him, of the slight smell of body sweat that was a heady aphrodisiac. She was seeing Gideon Steele as a man she was attracted to, and not as an adversary, and it was a dangerous emotion. She bit her lip. 'I—I was just on my way to the bathroom.'

'Feeling sick again?' His arm supported her as she walked to the adjoining bathroom.

'No,' she blushed.

'Oh,' he grinned. 'I'll leave you to it, then. Breakfast can wait.' he closed the door.

Merry looked in horror at the pale face, hollow eyes, and tangled hair that was her reflection in the mirror. Heavens, no wonder Gideon was still treating her like a delicate child—she looked awful! But thankfully the seasickness seemed to have faded, although she still couldn't say she liked the constant movement of the yacht.

She could hear Gideon whistling softly to himself as he waited for her, and she hurried through her wash, brushing her hair into some sort of order, although going to bed with it still wet from her shower had given it more curl than usual. She looked like a witch.

And to say she was surprised at Gideon's solicitous behaviour would be putting it mildly. She wouldn't have believed such an arrogantly selfish man could have been so nice to her. He had even tidied the bathroom for her, which, going by the disorder in his own cabin, he rarely did for himself, let alone anyone else.

But when had he left the comfort of her bed? Had he stayed with her all night or only part of it? What did it matter *how* long he had stayed with her, they had still shared a bed! The injection Michael had given her, as well as easing the nausea, had put her to sleep. But was sleep all that she had done in Gideon's arms? She had surely been in no condition to do anything else, although her memories of his body seemed rather too vivid if that had been the case!

He was lounging in an armchair when she joined him, but stood up to help her over to the table. 'I know you probably don't feel like eating,' he smiled at her grimace, 'but Michael says you're to eat a light breakfast and drink plenty of liquids.'

Just looking at the toast and coffee made her feel ill, but she could see the determined glint in Gideon's eyes as he sat opposite her. He poured coffee for them both.

'Don't let me keep you,' she told him awkwardly.

'You aren't,' he drawled.

She chewed uninterestedly on the piece of toast. 'I'm sure you would rather be up on deck, and not——'

'Not in here, alone, with my girl-friend?' he taunted. 'Don't be silly, Merry, any man would rather stay here with you. Everyone thinks I've come to spend the morning in bed with you too.'

'Too?' She paled at his first reference to the night she had just spent in his arms.

His brows arched. 'It seems to be commonly accepted that the reason you're staying in bed this morning is because of a lack of—sleep last night.'

Her hands clenched in her lap. 'And who gave them that impression?' she snapped.

He gave a lazy shrug, as he drank his coffee. 'Not me.'

'It's just a normal reaction for your women to be too exhausted to get out of bed after a night with you?'

An angry flush darkened the leanness of his cheeks. 'I think you're becoming insulting again, Merry.' His voice was dangerously soft.

She knew she was, but she was too angry to worry about Gideon's icy tone. 'You didn't have to let them think that, you could have told them——'

'What?' He stood up to glare down at her. 'You didn't want them to know you'd been ill.'

'I'd rather they knew that than think I——' She broke off as she realised how insulting that sounded. Gideon looked furious!

He wrenched her chin round, bending until his face was inches from her own. 'That you spent the night in bed with me, a night you swore only yesterday would never happen, not if I were the last man on earth?' he bit out softly. 'But you did, Merry,' his mouth twisted, 'and you enjoyed it too.'

'I——'

'You purred like a contented cat all night!' he flung her away from him, his whole body tense with anger. 'You may have been asleep, but your body was only too aware of its own wants and needs. And last night it wanted *me*!' he told her savagely.

She blanched. 'You didn't——'

'Didn't have sex with an unconscious woman?' he taunted harshly. 'I don't get my thrills that way. But it wasn't because of any objection from you!'

She wanted to deny his accusations, wanted to tell him he lied—and yet she couldn't. As soon as he had walked into her cabin this morning she had realised that she knew the hardness of his body almost as well as she knew her own.

She gave a distressed cry. 'I didn't know what I was doing!'

'No—but I knew,' he scorned. 'You aroused me last night, Merry. You kissed me and caressed me. *In your sleep*!'

'No!' she gasped.

'Yes,' Gideon bit out. 'And your hands and body

know *exactly* what they were doing to me.'

She put a hand up to her mouth, shaking. 'I didn't mean—I didn't—I've never——'

'I'm not so sure about that,' he rasped harshly. 'The way you touched me——'

'Don't keep talking about it!' she cried.

'All right, we won't talk about it,' he snapped. 'But I won't forget it either, Merry. I don't want to forget it.'

She blushed. 'I—I'd like to be alone now. I don't feel well.'

'No?' His mouth twisted. 'You're a woman, Merry, there's no shame in acting like one,' he added softly.

Her eyes flashed deeply green. 'And you should know,' she accused heatedly. 'Michael told me that almost every woman on this yacht has shared your bed in the past.'

'Not at the same time!' he ground out tauntingly.

Her blushes deepened. 'I didn't think—You're disgusting!'

'And Michael had no right to tell you anything about my personal life!'

'He was jealous——'

'Because of you?'

'No,' she sighed her impatience with such a suggestion. 'Because of Linda.'

'He had no need to be.' His mouth twisted. 'Linda is in love with him.'

'He seems to think she loves you.'

'Then he's a fool,' Gideon dismissed abruptly. 'Linda just likes to flirt, it doesn't mean anything. And I can't be answerable for what Michael *thinks*. Now, do you need any help getting back to bed?'

'No,' she choked.

'I don't intend joining you,' he taunted.

'You wouldn't have been invited to!'

'I had all the invitation I need from you last night,'

he mocked. 'And I didn't say no, just not yet. Remember that.' He closed the door quietly behind him as he left.

Merry began to shake with reaction, unable to remember everything about last night, but she remembered enough to know that he had a right to taunt her. She had behaved shamelessly in his arms, had clung to him, had explored the hard contours of his body until she felt him shudder with reaction.

And now he seemed to think she was a wanton, that she had known how her caresses would effect him, that she had wanted his lovemaking.

He was probably with Linda now, or one of the other beautiful women on board who smiled at him so invitingly. She didn't care, she told herself fiercely. As long as he stayed away from her!

She must have slept, although it was a restless sleep, vivid pictures of herself and Gideon flashing in and out of her mind. She was shaking when she woke up, and it was no longer due to seasickness.

She had dressed in a pale pink sun-dress, and was just brushing her hair before applying her make-up when a knock sounded on her cabin door. Gideon . . .! No, he never seemed to knock but simply walked straight in.

The door opened tentatively, and Anthea Steele looked inside the cabin, her expression brightening as she saw Merry was up and dressed. 'Can I come in?' she asked softly.

Merry swallowed hard, her make-up finished now. 'Please,' she nodded shyly.

The older woman came in and closed the door behind her, youthfully beautiful in a yellow bikini and matching robe, the latter tied casually about her slender waist. 'Feeling better?' she enquired as she sat on the edge of the bed Merry had already made, not being used to having people do things like that for her.

She frowned. 'Better . . .?'

Anthea smiled. 'Gideon told his father and me that you'd been ill in the night. It's all right,' she assured as Merry moaned her dismay, 'no one else knows. And I can sympathise, Merry,' she added warmly. 'I always get seasick myself.'

Merry's eyes widened. 'But you seem fine.'

'I am now,' the other woman laughed. 'I take tablets the first weeks, and then after that I'm usually acclimatised. You will be too after a few days.'

'I feel better already,' Merry admitted.

'That will please Gideon,' Anthea teased. 'He's been walking around like a bear with a sore head all morning!'

Colour flooded her cheeks. 'He's annoyed with me——'

'No,' Anthea dismissed. 'He's annoyed with himself, I think. He's sure you would have told him how ill you were feeling if you hadn't argued last night, and he blames himself.'

Merry shook her head. 'I'm sure you're wrong.'

'He told me so himself,' the other woman assured her. 'Now, would you like to come up deck for a while?'

'Is it rough?' She hesitated.

Anthea laughed, the shadows of last night no longer in evidence. 'It may seem that way to you . . .'

'But to you it's a millpond,' Merry said self-derisively.

'Yes,' the other woman smiled. 'The fresh air will help you feel better.'

'Merry, I——' Gideon stopped in the doorway, smiling warmly at his stepmother, his expression wary as he looked at Merry. 'How are you?' he asked huskily. He was wearing denims and a fitted brown shirt now.

If she hadn't known better she would have said his

concern was genuine, and he seemed to have done a good job of convincing his parents that it was. Anthea had been sure that guilt over her was the reason for his bad humour. But she knew it was really anger that put him in a bad mood—anger with her.

'Darling?' he prompted.

She started as she realised he was talking to her. 'I feel a lot better,' she told him stiffly, forgetting the part she was to play. This game was too dangerous for her.

He nodded. 'I looked in on you an hour ago, you were sleeping like a baby.'

Anthea stood up with a smile and walked to the door. 'I'll see you both in a few minutes.'

'Yes,' Gideon answered distractedly.

Merry turned back to the mirror to apply her lip-gloss, aware that she looked more human now, her blusher adding colour to her otherwise pale cheeks, her hair once again secured in the single plait down her spine.

But she was conscious of Gideon's reflection in the mirror, of being alone with him. 'I'm sorry——'

'I'm sorry——' they both began talking at the same time, and Gideon shrugged ruefully. 'You first,' he invited drily.

She put her make-up bag away and turned to him. 'I'm sorry about earlier,' she wetted her lips nervously. 'I realise I shouldn't have said what I did.'

'And I realise *I* shouldn't have said what I did either,' he grimaced. 'You were ill last night, you clung to me because I happened to be there. I—God, I'm not making a very good job of this,' he frowned. 'I didn't mean because I *happened* to be there, that doesn't sound right at all. I meant—Are you laughing, Merry?' he asked suspiciously.

She lowered her hand from her mouth, revealing that she was indeed laughing. It wasn't like Gideon to be at a loss for words, and yet he had made a complete mess of that apology. Luckily she knew exactly what he was trying to say, otherwise they might have been at each other's throats again by now. And she wasn't sure he was right anyway ...

She stood up to put her arm through the crook of his. 'Let's go up on deck,' she grinned at him, 'before you make matters any worse!'

He grimaced, opening the door. 'Could I?'

'Not much,' she laughed.

It was a beautifully clear day, the sun shining hotly, the sea a deep, deep blue. A gently breeze caught the loose tendrils of Merry's hair, carrying it across her mouth and face.

Gideon turned to gently brush it back, bending his head to kiss her lightly on the mouth. He smiled straight into her bemused green eyes as he raised his head. 'We have an audience,' he murmured.

She turned her head slightly, to see several of the yacht party sitting about on deck, some of them watching Gideon and herself with undisguised interest. She bent her head back to look up at him, the light of mischief in her eyes. 'I always play to an audience.' She raised herself on tiptoe to part his lips with her own, her arms clinging about his neck.

'It seems the lovers have made up,' drawled a sarcastic voice.

Merry instantly stiffened as she recognised that voice, but Gideon's arms about her kept her pressed against him, his lips parting even further as he deepened the kiss, exploring the erotic depths of her mouth with a thoroughness that left her gasping for air.

'After last night I needed that,' he told her throatily. 'Besides,' he added, pulling her firmly to his side with his arm about her waist, 'we have to keep the audience happy.'

The main 'audience' at the moment was Linda Martin, her sarcastic comment reflected in the hardness of her brown eyes. Gideon turned to the other woman with a smile, taking Merry down with him as he sank on to a lounger.

'That—display was quite wonderful, darling,' Linda drawled bitingly.

'I enjoyed it.' Gideon seemed unperturbed by the other woman's barb, looking over at the shaded area of the deck where a long trestle table was being laden with food. 'Lunch,' he said with satisfaction.

'You mean your—appetite isn't satisfied?' Linda snapped.

Merry gasped, but once again Gideon seemed unruffled by the other woman's show of jealousy. For jealousy was what it was. And the resigned-looking Michael lay on the lounger on Linda's other side, close enough to hear the intimacy of the conversation.

Gideon met the other woman's gaze steadily. 'I'm always hungry,' he drawled in the double-edged conversation, then turned pointedly to Merry. 'Are you coming with me to get the lunch, darling, or would you like me to bring you something back?'

'I'll come with you,' she said firmly, following him over to the buffet lunch where several people were already helping themselves to plates of food. There were lots of chickens, ham, beef, salmon, salad, and cold vegetables, just the sort of food suitable for such a hot day.

Gideon piled his plate high with the delicious food, although Merry put little on her own, as her appetite was still not very great. She didn't know how Gideon managed to stay so slim if he always ate like this.

'I work hard too,' he told her as he caught her glance.

'You would need to.' She nibbled on a chicken leg, glad that they had gone to one of the tables on deck and not back to where Linda still sat with the long-suffering Michael, the other couple seeming to have no interest in the food.

Gideon quirked one dark brow. 'How did it go with Anthea?' he asked seriously.

'We didn't talk for long,' she shrugged. 'But it seemed to be—fine.'

'Still a little uncertain about the commitment of telling her she's your mother?' His voice had lowered softly.

'A little,' she nodded, her gaze drawn to where Anthea sat at Samuel Steele's side, the two of them holding hands like young lovers.

Gideon followed her line of vision and his own expression softened. 'After her breakdown my father is more than ever aware of Anthea's importance in his life. I believe he would, quite literally, want to die without her,' he added huskily. 'It's beautiful, isn't it?'

'Yes,' Merry agreed without hesitation.

He pushed his plate away, empty now. 'And you dared to think *I* desired Anthea for myself!' His voice was harsh.

She swallowed her surprise at this attack. 'You—you knew?'

'Of course I knew,' he glared across the table at her. 'And I could quite cheerfully have hit you.'

Merry blushed, feeling his anger. 'How was I to know——'

'How were you not to know?' he rasped. 'I told you she was my mother——'

'You don't call her that!'

'Of course I don't,' he derided hardly. 'It would sound ridiculous. But in all the ways that matter she'd been my mother, my confidant, my friend. I can't expect you to understand that——'

'No, you can't, can you?' she choked, and turned

away, blinking back the tears that in her weakened condition she didn't seem able to control.

'Hell, Merry, I'm sorry!' He leant forward to clasp her hand. 'That was cruel of me——'

'Something you're good at!' she glared, wrenching her hand out of his. 'I think I'll go back down to my cabin, I'm feeling tired.'

Gideon's mouth was tight. 'I'll come with you.'

'No!' she snapped. 'Go and join Linda, I'm sure she'll be glad of your company!'

Anger flared fiercely in the deep blue eyes. 'What the hell is the matter with you, Merry? I spoke without thinking, I've apologised for that. There's no need for you to go off in a damned sulk.'

'I'm not sulking,' she stood up noisily. 'Just tired of your company.'

His breath caught angrily in his throat at her rudeness, but before he could make a cutting remark back she had turned on her heel, going in the direction of the stairs down to her cabin. She almost groaned her dismay as Linda stepped in her way. This woman's taunts were the last thing she wanted right now; her own thoughts were too confused and chaotic for her to control her temper.

'Argued again, have you?' Linda drawled mockingly, the bright red bikini she wore only just covering her voluptuous body, her sexuality tangible even to Merry.

Her mouth tightened. 'What business is it of yours, Miss Martin?' her voice was huskily soft.

The other woman shrugged, leaning on the rail to make a show of admiring their tranquilly beautiful surroundings. But her eyes were hard as she looked back at Marry. 'Gideon doesn't like difficult women,' she mocked. 'he simply doesn't care enough to make the chase.'

'Thank you for the advice,' Merry taunted.

'Oh, it isn't advice,' Linda gave a hard smile. 'It's just the simple truth. Push Gideon too far and you'll find he simply gives up and goes after another quarry.'

'You?'

The other woman wet the full redness of her lips with a provocation that made Merry squirm with indignation. 'Perhaps,' she nodded.

'And your fiancé?'

Linda shrugged. 'Will still be my fiancé. I don't have any illusions about Gideon. He'll never marry, could never make that commitment to one woman.'

'And while you're being Gideon's latest—quarry, you expect Michael to just sit back and wait until you've had your little fling?' Marry's mouth twisted contemptuously.

Hard brown eyes narrowed. 'Why not?'

Merry glanced over to where Michael seemed to have fallen asleep, his body lean and firmly muscled. He was probably a little older than Gideon now that she could see him in the daylight, but he was no less attractive for all that.

She turned back to Linda. 'If you decide on Gideon let me know,' she drawled. 'Michael might be worth—cultivating.' Linda's indignant gasp was lost to her as she strolled off with a cool confidence.

It was a different matter once she reached the cool sanctuary of her own cabin and sat down heavily on the bed. Her bravado might have made her feel better, but she had no doubt there would be reprisals. The worst of it was she didn't know why she had really done it. She felt so angry all the time, with everyone, especially Gideon.

As if thinking of him had conjured him up her cabin door opened and he walked inside, slamming the door behind him. She could tell by the furious glitter of his eyes that he hadn't forgiven her for her latest insult.

He came to stand in front of her, legs apart in challenge, the muscled tautness of his thighs on a level with her eyes. 'What do you mean by telling Linda you'll take on Michael if she wants me?' he rasped.

Merry gasped. Her reprisal had come in a form she hadn't anticipated, and her eyes widened on the harsh fury of Gideon's face, a nerve beating erratically in his cheek. She swallowed hard. 'I didn't exactly say that.'

'No?'

She touched her lips nervously with the tip of her tongue. 'No, I——'

'God, girl, you're driving me insane!' Gideon ground out, dropping to her side on the bed, his extra weight making her dip in his direction, falling into his arms. 'Do that to me,' he groaned.

She was breathing heavily, her face showing her bewilderment. 'Do what to you?'

'That!' he moaned as her tongue once again flicked nervously over lips. 'Touch me like that, Merry.'

'Gideon . . .!'

'For God's sake!' he trembled against her, his arms steely as he bent her to his will, capturing and parting her lips, his mouth moving with erotic pleasure over hers, willing that provocative movement of her tongue.

Her head was spinning, conscious only of the warm seduction of Gideon's body against hers, and she offered no resistance as he pushed her gently back on the bed, his thighs and legs half covering her as he told her of his rapidly rising desire.

She felt as if she were drowning in the blue depths of his eyes, her breathing shallow now, as if she were afraid to break the dream.

'Please!' he groaned. 'I've been burning for you since last night. That kiss earlier just wasn't enough. I need your touch, Merry!'

Of their own volition her arms encircled his neck,

pulling him down to her the necessary distance to outline his parted lips with the tip of her tongue, and she felt him shudder against her before he captured her lips, nothing gentle about his kiss as he plundered her mouth. She felt him tremble as she caressed his body as she had in her sleep, last night, revelling in her consciousness, in the hard strength of him.

His hands moved restlessly over her body, filling her with a burning ache, raising her to fever-pitch, offering no words of protest as she felt his fingers probe the two buttons at the top of her breasts that held the shoulder-straps of the sun-dress in place, pulling the material down to her waist to expose her bare breasts.

He expelled a shuddering breath as he looked down at her, the deep red nipples already erect and begging for the hungry caress of his mouth. He slid slowly down her body, his lips a pleasure-giving flame as he caught the nipple between his teeth, flicking the hardened nub with his tongue.

Merry's fingers dug into his scalp, holding him to her as the desire flooded her body. Gideon gave a groan of male pleasure, his lips moving to the other breast as his hand continued the caress of the nipple he had just left.

Merry moved restlessly beneath him, her limbs melting with a desire she had never known before, her fingers moving to unbutton his shirt, loving the smooth dampness of his chest and back, licking his salty skin.

Suddenly he buried his face in her throat, heavy above her. 'This is insane,' he muttered. '*I'm* insane!' he raised his head to look down at her, the flush of desire still in the hardness of his cheeks. 'If only you hadn't made that stupid taunt to Linda,' he groaned.

She instantly stiffened, her own desire fading. 'What taunt?' she queried softly.

He swung away from her, running a rueful hand through the dark thickness of his hair, paying no attention to Merry's fumbling movements with her dress. 'About Michael,' he grimaced.

She sat up, pushing back the plait that had fallen over her shoulder, untidy wisps of hair now feathered about her flushed face. 'What makes you think it was a stupid taunt?'

He turned to look at her sharply, the dark hair on his chest short and wiry. 'What do you mean?'

She shrugged, wanting to stand up, to break away from him completely, but she was afraid her legs wouldn't carry her. 'If you go off with Linda——'

'Which I won't!' he ground out.

'Then Michael will be on his own and so will I,' she continued as if he hadn't interrupted. 'Pride dictates that I would have to—become friends with Michael.'

Gideon was the one to stand up, glaring down at her as he buttoned his shirt. 'I just told you I have no intention of going after Linda!'

Her mouth twisted, feeling more sure of herself without his warmth next to her. 'You wouldn't need to,' she derided. 'Just hold out your hand to her!'

His mouth tightened angrily. 'I don't want to "hold out my hand to her",' he snapped.

Merry was too disturbed at the moment to understand the warmth that flooded through her at this claim. 'Then just wait for her to come to you,' she taunted. 'It shouldn't be long.'

'Maybe you should remember that you aren't really my girl-friend, that this is all pretence,' he bit out as he tucked his shirt back into his trousers.

Merry paled, holding on to her composure with effort. 'What do you mean?'

'Your attitude to Linda is like that of a jealous girl-friend,' he snapped.

'Isn't that what I'm supposed to be?'

'Not when we're alone!'

Love, romance, intrigue...all are captured for you by Mills & Boon's top-selling authors.
TAKE FOUR EXCITING BOOKS ABSOLUTELY FREE

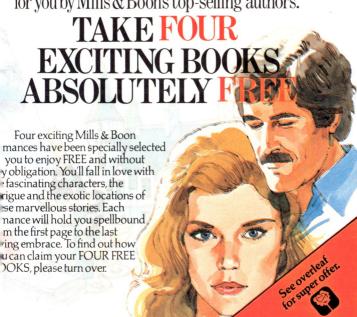

Four exciting Mills & Boon romances have been specially selected for you to enjoy FREE and without any obligation. You'll fall in love with the fascinating characters, the intrigue and the exotic locations of these marvellous stories. Each romance will hold you spellbound from the first page to the last loving embrace. To find out how you can claim your FOUR FREE BOOKS, please turn over.

See overleaf for super offer.

Do not affix postage stamps if posted in Gt. Britain, Channel Islands or N. Ireland.

BR LICENCE NO. CN81

Mills & Boon Reader Service, PO Box 236, CROYDON, Surrey CR9 9EL.

2

Mills & Boon, the world's most popular publisher of romantic fic **invites you to take these four books free.**

FOUR BOOKS FREE

As a special introductory offer to the Mills & Boon Reader Service, we will send you four superb Mills & Boon Romances ABSOLUTELY FREE and WITHOUT OBLIGATIO Become a subscriber, and you will receive each month:

- THE NEWEST ROMANCES – reserved at the printers and delivered direct to you b Mills & Boon.

- POSTAGE AND PACKING FREE – you only pay the same as you would in the shop

- NO COMMITMENT – you receive books only for as long as you want.

- FREE MONTHLY NEWSLETTER – keeps you up-to-date with new books and book bargains.

- HELPFUL, FRIENDLY SERVICE from the girls at Mills & Boon. You can ring us any time on 01-684 2141.

THE FOUR FREE BOOKS SHOWN HERE ARE OUR SPECIAL GIFT TO YOU. THEY ARE YOURS TO KEEP REGARDLESS OF WHETHER YOU WISH TO BUY FURTHER BOOKS.

Just fill in and post the coupon today.

Mills & Boon

Mills & Boon Reader Service, PO Box 236, Croydon, Surrey CR9 3RU.

NO STAMP NEEDED

FREE BOOKS CERTIFICATE

To: Mills & Boon Reader Service, PO Box 236, Croydon, Surrey CR9 9EL.

Please send me, free and without obligation the four Mills & Boon Romances illustrated in this leaflet, and reserve a Reader Service Subscription for me. If I decide to subscribe I shall, from the beginning of the month following my free parcel of books, receive six new books each month for £5.70 post and packing free. If I decide not to subscribe, I shall write to you within 14 days. The free books are mine to keep in any case.
I understand that I may cancel my subscription at any time simply by writing to you. I am over 18 years of age.

Please write in BLOCK CAPITALS

Name_____

Address_____

_____

_____ Post Code_____

SEND NO MONEY – TAKE NO RISKS.   10R 36

One offer per household. Offer applies in UK only – overseas send for details. If price changes are necessary you will be notif

Her breath caught in her throat. 'I wasn't alone with you when I made those remarks to Linda, and her taunts were rather too pointed to ignore.'

Gideon's eyes were narrowed. 'So you didn't mean it about Michael?'

'I didn't say that,' she said slowly.

He marched over with long angry strides to pull her roughly to her feet. 'You will stay away from him, Merry. Do you hear me?' he shook her.

'I—I hear you,' she nodded, relieved when the shaking stopped.

Once again his eyes narrowed. 'I don't like it when you agree too easily, it usually means you're up to something,' he muttered.

Her mouth twisted. 'I'm sure you credit me with more deviousness than I possess.'

'And I'm equally sure I don't,' he derided, putting her away from him. 'You may look like a child, but your thoughts and actions are those of a woman. Okay, I'll give you the benefit of the doubt—for now. But stay away from Michael, or risk the consequences.'

She frowned at him suspiciously. 'Consequences? What consequences?'

'You'll have to wait and see, won't you?' he taunted softly. 'But I wouldn't advise it. I'll see you later, when you've had your rest.'

'Going to be with Linda?' Merry couldn't resist this last barb.

Gideon stopped at the door, turning slowly. 'If I am it's none of your concern. Like I said, you aren't really my girl-friend.' The door closed softly behind him.

The tension left Merry's body with a sigh. No, she wasn't really his girl-friend, but a few minutes ago she had almost become his lover. Now she knew the reason for her anger, with everyone, including herself.

She had fallen in love with Gideon Steele!

CHAPTER SIX

How could you fall in love with a man you didn't even like very much? Merry didn't know *how*, she just knew she had done it. It was ridiculous, even stupid, to have allowed this to happen, and yet she knew she loved him.

She had shared more with Gideon than with any other man, had shown him the lash of her temper, had been rude to him, had been ill in front of him, had shared a bed with him, had almost made love with him. The latter, she knew, hadn't been stopped by any reluctance on her part; Gideon had been in complete control of that.

She was stuck on this yacht for almost another two weeks with a man she knew she was in love with! And there was no possibility of him ever loving her in return. She hadn't needed Linda Martin's warning to tell her what sort of man Gideon was, she already knew he had only contempt for most women.

She knew that his lovemaking of just now had only been evoked by the close proximity of last night, that she had forced that situation on him. Gideon was a sensual man, and her encouragement had aroused him.

She couldn't face him at the moment, spending most of the afternoon in her cabin, with only a visit from Michael to alleviate her boredom. But she daren't go up on deck and see Gideon, not when she was feeling so vulnerable.

'How do you feel now?' Michael sat down next to her.

'A lot better,' she smiled. 'I don't know what you gave me, but it works!'

He grinned. 'It's supposed to. No after-effects?'

'Just tiredness,' she grimaced, knowing that she couldn't sleep, not now.

'You don't feel like soaking up some of the sunshine?'

She avoided his gaze. 'Not just now.'

Michael stood up. 'I'd better get back on deck—before Gideon decides to persuade Linda she's made a mistake in agreeing to marry me!'

The words were spoken lightly, and yet Merry could sense an underlying strain in his tone. 'He wouldn't do that,' she assured him.

'No,' Michael agreed heavily, 'I don't suppose he would.'

She could still see the tension in his eyes. 'Perhaps I will come up on deck after all,' she said brightly. 'I'll just get some shoes.' She could see Michael wasn't at all sure about Gideon!

Neither was she, when she got up on deck to find him stretched out on a lounger next to Linda, his only clothing a pair of navy blue swimming trunks that left little to the imagination. The colour faded from Merry's cheeks as she remembered how close she had come to knowing the full possession of that muscled body.

Gideon turned in their direction as she and Michael walked towards them, the expression in his eyes hidden behind dark sunglasses, although his mouth tightened at Michael's hand on her arm. To Merry's relief she felt some of the old resentment surge through her at this arrogant display of ownership. How dared he look at *her* so accusingly!

'Been making house-calls, darling?' Linda drawled to her fiancé as they reached them.

'Cabin-calls,' he corrected, seeing Merry seated before sitting down himself. 'I managed to persuade Merry to join us.'

'How nice!' the other woman taunted.

All this time Merry had been conscious of Gideon's brooding silence, his head turned in her direction, although the sunglasses prevented her from telling what he was thinking. She took her own sunglasses out of her bag and pushed them pointedly on to her nose. Damn him!

When Michael suggested that he and Linda take a walk around the deck Merry looked up in dismay. She didn't want to be alone with Gideon right now. Linda agreed to the walk, although Merry treated sceptically the other woman's comment about walking off some of the calories, her figure already perfect.

The silence between Gideon and herself was even more noticeable and oppressive now that they were alone, and Merry shifted uncomfortably, acknowledging Anthea's smile and wave across the deck with a nervous movement of her hand.

She was conscious of everything about Gideon, wondering how he had, seemingly, managed to get that all-over tan, with no white skin visible on his body anywhere.

'Naked sunbathing,' he suddenly drawled mockingly.

Her lids flew upwards and she found Gideon's head turned in her direction. How long had he been aware of her gaze on him! Two wings of colour heightened her cheeks as she answered him. 'I beg your pardon?' she frowned.

'I got the tan by sunbathing naked.' He sat up. 'That's what you were wondering, weren't you?'

She caught her top lip between her teeth. 'I—Yes,' she admitted.

'Well, now you know,' he taunted, his mouth tightening. 'I warned you to stay away from Michael.'

Merry's eyes flashed her indignation, although she doubted he was aware of that, her own sunglasses being as effective as his. 'I did stay away from him,' she snapped. 'He came to see me—on a professional basis.'

'He was gone a damned long time,' Gideon rasped.

'Ten minutes at most,' she defended heatedly.

'Ten minutes too damned long,' he insisted grimly. 'What did he have to say?'

'That the sunshine will do me good.'

'Hm,' his gaze raked over her. 'Why don't you put on a bikini and get a tan?'

And feel naked in front of him! With her newly made discovery she didn't feel confident enough to cope with that. 'I think I'll go and talk to your father and Anthea.' She stood up, smoothing down her dress.

Gideon caught hold of her wrist and got slowly to his feet. 'I'll come with you.'

'You have no need——'

'I want to.' He took her hand in his. 'I want to, Merry.'

There was no answer she could make to that, and how she controlled the shiver of pleasure his hand evoked she never knew. The warm pressure of that hand remained firmly closed around hers as they talked with his parents, Samuel Steele proving to have a dry wit that Merry felt drawn to, while Anthea's admiration and love for her husband was obvious.

Merry noticed that both men treated the other woman as a delicate child, and she could see that although Anthea loved them both in return she found this over-protectiveness a little irksome at times. Finally Gideon challenged his father to a game of chess, and the two of them disappeared into the lounge. Merry wondered if Gideon had deliberately taken the other man away to allow her time with her mother, finally deciding he had.

'Neither of them like to lose,' Anthea grimaced. She had discarded her wrap now, and was just wearing the bikini. Merry was beginning to feel slightly overdressed!

'Who usually wins?' she smiled.

'It varies,' the other woman told her. 'Depending on which one is feeling the most aggressive at the time.'

'In that case, it will probably be Gideon,' she said dryly.

Anthea levelled green eyes on her, and Meredith felt relieved that her identical green eyes were shielded behind the sunglasses. It was strange to look into eyes so like her own, a *face* so like her own if you knew of the connection between them. And she did; she knew there could never be any doubt that Anthea was her mother.

But Anthea didn't know. Her gaze was friendly, but nothing more. 'I thought the two of you were friends again?'

Friends? Merry and Gideon could never be friends. Adversaries, yes, even lovers, but never friends. 'I'm afraid I've been a little bad-tempered since we arrived yesterday. I think it was the journey, and then the seasickness last night,' she invented.

'Probably,' the other woman sympathised.

'And you?' Merry probed gently. 'Gideon told me you hadn't been well.' She could hardly get to know her mother if they remained polite strangers!

Anthea frowned. 'He did?'

'Yes,' she nodded.

Anthea flushed, obviously unsure as to why her stepson should have told his young girl-friend about that. 'It was last year,' she dismissed with forced lightness. 'I'm completely well now.'

Merry hadn't missed the shadows that had come back into the other woman's eyes, and she wished now that she hadn't mentioned the illness. 'Are you?' she said huskily.

'Of course.' Anthea's voice was brittle. 'Come and say hello to some of the others. I'm not sure if Gideon introduced you last night.'

She had met most of the other twenty or so guests, although she went along with the other woman to renew the acquaintance, enjoying the next hour or so.

It was Gideon who had the triumphant look on his face when the two men rejoined them, and she and Anthea shared a smile of acknowledgment. It felt good to share something with her mother, even if it were only gentle mockery of Gideon.

His challenge and defeat over his father seemed to have put him in a good mood, his manner to Merry was friendly and teasing, something she felt glad of. She was too vulnerable to withstand his barbs right now.

They arrived in Turkey the next day, in the port of Izmir, a strangely modern city, a mixture of the beautiful and the unusual. Merry saw all of this as she and Gideon took a taxi south from the harbour.

He had casually informed her at breakfast, a totally informal affair on deck, helping themselves to food from the platters set out on the tables, that he was taking her to Ephesus today! 'There's a lot to see at Izmir,' he turned to tell her dryly, during a break in the Turkish taxi-driver's excited monologue of the city. 'But I think Ephesus is the most interesting. And Michael said you shouldn't be out too long today.'

'Michael did?' Her eyes widened; her hair hung free down her back today, her cotton top was loose and cool, her denims fitted snugly.

Gideon's face darkened, a startling contrast to his good humour the evening before. His mood of gentle teasing had persisted last night, and for a while Merry had forgotten her tension with him, had allowed herself the luxury of thinking he actually did like her and didn't just tolerate her. But his frown now brought all the wariness back, and with it the futility of loving a man like Gideon. It wasn't fair that this blue-eyed devil of a man should be the one she loved.

'He is your doctor on this trip,' Gideon rasped.

'Oh—oh yes,' she blushed. 'I'd forgotten,' she admitted.

'Really?' His voice was icy now. 'I would advise you not to think of him as anything else. Your interest in him has only made Linda all the more determined to hang on to him.'

'That's something, at least! Jealous because of that, Gideon?' she taunted.

'Not at all,' he answered easily, glancing out of the window. 'Just warning you. I wouldn't want you to get hurt.'

Merry was very aware of the taxi-driver's silence as she and Gideon spoke in low, heated voices, sensing the man's interest in them in the driving mirror. He was a short, stocky Turk, with a manner that liked to please. He was obviously dismayed by what he took to be an argument between his customers, possibly imagining he would lose his fare if they argued too badly and demanded to go back to the yacht.

'I won't get hurt, Gideon,' she told him softly. At least, not by Michael!

'Good,' his tone was abrupt.

'What's at Ephesus?' She changed the subject, wishing for the return of the lighthearted companion from breakfast.

He smiled, some of the anger leaving him. 'What's at Ephesus?' he derided.

Unfortunately, before he could follow up the taunt, the driver, thinking he had been asked the question, launched into a list and description of the places of interest at Selçuk, the small modern town that had grown up near Ephesus, a ruined city remaining from the time of Alexander the Great. Gideon and Merry shared an amused smile and let the man continue, knowing he was enjoying himself.

By the time the man had finished Merry's head was spinning with tales of the first Ephesus, named after an Amazon queen, built about 3000 B.C., of the second city 1000 B.C., and the last one, the one that still remained, in the fourth century B.C. It seemed incredible to her that a whole city, even a ruined one, could still remain after all that time.

Before she could voice her scepticism, the driver told them of the other interests of Selçuk, the Basilica of St John, of the Isa Bey Mosque, and the Temple of Artemis, or Diana.

'We'll only go to those if we have time,' Gideon told the man abruptly.

They drove for over an hour. The countryside was sometimes flat, sometimes mountainous, but always beautiful. The roadside was a splendour of green vegetation, flat plains leading up to mountains. Merry hadn't imagined Turkey looked like this at all, and she now knew the full meaning of travelling broadening the mind.

Gideon instructed the driver to meet them at the other entrance once they reached Ephesus. 'It's quite a walk,' he told Merry after paying over the money to enter the site. 'I don't think you'll want to walk back once we get to the other end.'

She walked at his side, glad she had put on sensible shoes, allowing him to hold her elbow on the unevenness of the pathway that led to the start of the city. The ground then became grassy before it gave way to stone slabs. 'How can you be sure the driver won't just turn around and go back to Izmir without us?' she mocked his arrogance.

Gideon grinned. 'Quite easily, I haven't paid him yet.'

'Oh!' she laughed.

'Incentive enough to keep him waiting, I would think,' he drawled.

'Yes,' she smiled, looking at her guide book to tell her the name of the building that used to exist where only glistening white pillars now stood in glorious spendour along the entrance of the Odeion, the council hall of the city. It was a fantastic building, a half circle of seats like those in a theatre today.

On the left-hand side of them as they turned the corner on to the stone-slabbed street stood a temple, dedicated to the Roman Emperor Domitian, her guide book said. But it was the street that held her awed attention, a long stretch of slab flooring going slightly downhill, with high pillars either side, with several statues amongst them. She and Gideon walked down the slow incline, the slabs beneath their feet worn with age and use.

Merry was lost in the beauty that surrounded her, and had forgotten Gideon as she stopped to look at the Temple of Hadrian, the same Hadrian from Athens, the layers of houses on the hillside opposite the temple seeming to actually be built into the hill itself, although they could just possibly have been excavated that way and left.

They had passed the Roman Baths on their way in, and now they passed the Baths of Scholastikia, which had a steam room, a warm bath, and then the cold bath. It was very like taking a sauna and then a cold swim nowadays.

'They seem to be obsessed with baths,' she murmured to Gideon, almost afraid to break the silence, although there were several other people wandering around the ruins too.

'Why not?' he shrugged. 'They had five springs flowing into the area, so they had no shortage of water.

A very civilised people, the Romans. They even had a very effective drainage system.'

They had passed the hillside houses now, and turned into another main street. Merry attempted to find the building to her right in the guide-book. She couldn't find it, and she walked towards the board that would tell her the name of this curious-looking building. It seemed to have one main room with several other rooms all leading off it, some of them with mosaic floors.

'The brothel,' Gideon supplied before she reached the board.

She had just got close enough to read that for herself, and a deep blush coloured her cheeks. 'So I see,' she muttered.

'At least, that's what they think it was. And over here,' he crossed the marble road, 'is the library.'

'How cultural,' she drawled.

He gave a husky laugh. 'Beats reading any day!'

She ignored him, and stood admiring the library. It was the most impressive building she had seen so far, seeming to have the frontage mainly intact, the two-storied pillars still standing, the stonework ornate, with several perfect statues standing in tall niches.

'Like I said,' Gideon shrugged, 'a clever people. A pity about the decadence. Have you seen the marble paving beneath us? Amazing,' he said in admiration.

The flat slabs of stone had given way to marble paving, glistening whitely in the sunlight. In fact it was a deceptively hot day, and Merry had made no objection when they got out of the car and Gideon pushed her white sunhat on to her head, welcoming the shade it offered. The soft breeze gave the impression of coolness, and yet she was aware of her arms becoming a golden brown as the day progressed.

'You have freckles on your nose too,' Gideon told

her as they approached the theatre, once again seeming to read her mind with unerring accuracy. A dangerous pastime—for her.

'I do?' She put up a hand selfconsciously to her face and blushed.

'You do,' he grinned. 'And they're very tempting.'

'Tempting?' She looked up at him with wide eyes.

'To do this.' He moved closer to her, kissing the tip of her nose before his mouth moved down to capture her lips. 'This seems almost sacrilegious,' he murmured ruefully at their surroundings, taking her arm to help her down on to the dirt platform of the theatre. 'Although I'm sure the Romans would understand.' Once again he took her into his arms. 'I want you quite shamelessly, Miss Charles,' he told her huskily.

His words were confusing enough, but the fact that he had said them in the theatre, the half-circular styling of the seats giving it wonderful acoustics, meant that the other people looking around the theatre had heard the softly spoken words too.

Colour flooded Merry's cheeks as they became the centre of attention, but Gideon merely chuckled as he released her, acknowledging the indulgent looks in their direction with a slight inclination of his dark head. But Merry made her exit as quickly as possibly, and was almost at the exit by the time Gideon's long stride caught up with her.

'Slow down,' he ordered lazily, grasping her arm to pull her to his side as they strolled out of the site towards the stalls selling goods, from clothes to the inevitable tourist gimmicks.

'But they all *heard*!' she groaned her embarrassment.

His eyes narrowed. 'And is it so important to you that they did?'

'Yes,' she hissed.

'I see,' his hand dropped away. 'Then forget I said it.'

Forget it? How could she forget it? Gideon had told her that he wanted her, Gideon who preferred to treat her as a child, who told her she *was* a child!

He maintained a stony silence as they wandered through the market stalls, making Merry so uncomfortable that she gave up looking at the beautiful vases and clothes and suggested they leave.

'You look tired,' Gideon told her abruptly as they found their driver and got back into the taxi.

She felt tired, her lack of sleep from two nights ago, and her lack of appetite for food yesterday and today meant she had a distinct lack of energy. But not for anything would she have told him of these feelings of weakness.

'I feel fine,' she said brightly. 'What's next on the agenda?'

'Take us back to the yacht,' Gideon instructed the driver—who looked very disappointed by their lack of interest in seeing the other interests here.

'But——'

'The yacht,' Gideon firmly interrupted Merry's protest.

She gave him a resentful glare, sure that he blamed her for cutting short their day. But she was feeling tired, and a glance at her wrist-watch told her they had been wandering round the ruins of Ephesus for almost two hours! Gideon had been right, she wouldn't have liked to have had to make the walk back.

The yacht was deserted when they arrived back, and she and Gideon ate their lunch alone, a delicious chicken and prawn salad followed by fresh fruit.

'I think you should rest now,' he told her after they had eaten, her appetite still not fully recovered.

She looked at him uncertainly, knowing a lie-down was exactly what she needed. 'What will you do?' She hesitated.

Blue eyes looked at her coldly, ice in their depths. 'Don't worry about me. I'm sure I can find something to amuse me,' he taunted.

'Or someone,' she snapped.

His mouth tightened. 'If I felt in need of that sort of amusement I'd join you in your cabin.'

'You damn well wouldn't!' she flared.

'No?' Dark brows rose, his hand moving caressingly up her arm. 'Oh, I think I would,' he drawled as he felt her pleasurable response to his touch.

Merry stood up, pushing her chair back noisily. 'I think I'll go and rest now.'

His mouth twisted in a caricature of a smile. 'You do that. And have pleasant dreams.'

Her dreams were all of him—as he had known they would be, damn him! She awoke with a start, bewildered for a moment by her surroundings, lying back with a sigh as she remembered where she was. And why she was here! Far from getting to know her mother she had fallen in love with Gideon. And the fact that he now admitted to wanting her bore no resemblance to that love. She had been a fool, a stupid fool.

The yacht still seemed very quiet, and a glance at her watch told her it was almost five o'clock. She had slept for three hours! Surely the others would be returning soon. And what about Gideon? She doubted he had expected to be left to his own devices for this long.

She got up to wash and change into a flowered skirt and pale blue tee-shirt, brushing her hair loose before going up on deck. She had acquired a golden tan on their trip out this morning, her skin glowing with health, the sleep erasing any last feelings of sickness. She hoped she wouldn't have a recurrence of it once they set sail again this evening!

The deck was deserted, as were the loungers, and a

brief knock on Gideon's cabin door elicited no answer either. Where on earth was he?

Her lips curved into a smile of relief as she came up on deck again and saw a familiar face. 'Niko!' she laughed.

'Miss Charles,' he returned her greeting with his usual good humour. 'You are all alone, hmm?' he sympathised.

She grimaced. 'It looks like it. Er—Have you seen Gideon?' She made her tone as casual as possible.

Niko's smile faded. 'He is in Cesme. You not know this?'

She frowned. 'Cesme? What's that? Part of the yacht?'

He shook his head. 'It is eighty kilometres, about fifty miles, from here.'

The colour left her face, leaving her looking young and bewildered. 'And Gideon's—gone there?' she asked hesitantly.

'*Ne*—yes,' he repeated in English. 'Is nice there. Sand, the sea. You know?'

Yes, she did now. And Gideon had gone off and left her all alone here. 'Did he take anyone with him?' she asked casually.

'No,' he stood his head. 'But Mr and Mrs Steele already there. Other guests too.'

Including Linda? She felt sure of it. 'Thank you, Niko,' she dismissed heavily.

'You like a drink?' he encouraged. 'Fruit juice? Some of your English tea, perhaps?'

Merry could see he was trying to please her, that he sensed her disappointment at Gideon's absence, accepting some of the latter, smiling brightly as she took some postcards out of her bag to write on the back of them, eager to show him she wasn't bothered by Gideon going to Cesme. She doubted she had convinced Niko, but it salved her pride a little.

She was relaxing on one of the loungers, her postcards written, when the others began to come back on board, several of them stopping to talk to her, sympathising with her tiredness—the reason Gideon must have given for her not accompanying him, she supposed. Gideon was almost the last on board, laughing huskily at something Linda was saying to him, the unhappy-looking Michael trailing along behind them.

Gideon's eyes narrowed as Merry got up and went down to her cabin before he reached her. She couldn't face him now; she knew exactly how poor Michael felt, her own love making her as vulnerable to Gideon as he was to Linda.

She half expected Gideon to berate her for her deliberate snub, but he made no reference to it when they met for dinner, was very attentive to her throughout the meal, a fact that took a little getting used to.

Linda made some effort to get his attention after the meal as they watched their departure from Turkey, but Gideon politely refused to leave Merry's side. Tonight one of the lounges was used to dance, soft romantic music filtering through the intercom system.

'Merry?' Gideon stood up to hold out his hand to her invitingly.

She hesitated only slightly, moving into the haven of his arms, making no demur as he rested her head on his shoulder. It was too relaxing to fight him, too—too wonderful, to want to question his motives for being so attentive.

They danced on in silence for over an hour, Gideon holding her tightly to him, making her aware of the rigid hardness of his body, his breath warm on her temple as he rested his head against hers.

Merry's arms clung loosely about his neck as she

swayed in time to the music, aware that their apparent absorption in each other was causing more than a ripple of interest. And Linda looked ready to do her some physical injury, finally settling for tormenting Michael with the seduction of her body as they too danced. Merry watched the movement of the other woman against Michael, wishing she dared be that provocative with Gideon. But he would probably laugh at her.

'You can if you want to,' he suddenly murmured against her ear.

She raised startled eyes to his, hating the way he seemed to read her mind while she could tell nothing of his thoughts. 'Can what?' she delayed, wetting her lips nervously.

He smiled down at her, very dark and predatory in the dimmed lighting. 'Move against me like that,' he said huskily. 'I can't promise to have the same forbearance as Michael seems to be having——'

'As *you* wouldn't have if I were Linda!' she snapped, cursing her jealousy, hating the ugly emotion. She was usually strong-willed, freely admitted to having a temper, but she didn't usually behave like a shrew. She seemed to have done nothing else lately.

Gideon continued to smile. 'Aren't you aware of your own attraction?'

She blushed. 'I couldn't hope to compete with Linda.'

'No one is asking you to,' he mocked. 'Linda isn't the sort of woman you can relax with——'

'Meaning I'm boring, I suppose!' she glared up at him.

'How you love to lose your temper,' he mused softly. 'And how beautiful you look when you do,' he added seriously. 'Thought any more about what I said this morning?'

She looked away. 'You said a lot of things this morning,' she evaded.

Gideon shook his head. 'No, I didn't.'

No, he hadn't, he had been very quiet today, which was how she knew exactly what he was talking about. Of course she had thought about him wanting her, but wanting wasn't the same as loving. Maybe if she just wanted him too she might be able to accept the affair he had been asking for, but she didn't just want him, and she had never been one to settle for half measures in anything.

'Well?' He watched her with narrowed eyes.

'I'm too young for you, remember?' she said lightly.

'And I'm too old for you,' he nodded. 'Unfortunately my body wants you, it *aches* for you,' he added huskily.

She felt a fluttering sensation in her breast, and closed her eyes to shut out the seduction of him. 'Fortunately I have more control over mine,' she told him coolly.

Gideon seemed unimpressed. 'So you *can* act,' he taunted softly.

She swallowed hard, knowing that her inexperience with dealing with situations like this made it impossible for her to keep up her façade of sophistication. And Gideon saw straight through it anyway!

'Come to my cabin,' he encouraged at her lack of denial. 'We can—talk about this further there.'

Talking sounded like the last thing Gideon had on his mind, and she pulled away from him. 'I think I'd like a drink,' she told him breathlessly.

His mouth twisted. 'Coward!'

'It's better than being a flirt!' she flashed at him as they sat down.

He shrugged. 'I can't see what your problem is. I want you, you want me, we're both consenting adults, and—Ah,' he sighed as he saw her blush, 'I was right at the Parthenon, I have come across that rare commodity, a virgin.' His eyes were narrowed.

Wild colour flooded her cheeks at the derision in his tone. 'We aren't rare,' she snappedl 'At least, not amongst *my* friends.'

'Bitchy!' he drawled. 'I think I made a mistake bringing you here as my girl-friend, Merry.'

'I'm sure you did!'

'Hm,' he nodded, sipping the whisky the steward had brought him. 'But now I'm stuck with you.'

'Thank you!' she choked, her own glass of pineapple juice landing with a thud on the table. 'I'm sorry if I cramp your style.'

'You do,' he drawled. 'My father reminded me only this afternoon that you are my guest, my responsibility.'

'Your father did?' Merry gasped, beginning to realise the reason for his attentiveness this evening.

'Yes,' he nodded. 'I hadn't realised when I made the suggestion of your being my girl-friend that I would be expected to spend all my time with you.'

Merry had had enough, and picked up her evening bag in preparation to leave. 'I'm sorry I'm not willing to provide the—entertainment you crave,' her voice shook with anger, 'but I'll leave you to find someone who will. I'm sure any number of your ex-girl-friends here would be more than happy to oblige.'

'I told you,' Gideon drawled, 'it's you or nothing on this trip. Parental instructions,' he derided harshly.

'Then it's nothing!' Her eyes flashed. 'Excuse me.' And she turned and walked proudly out of the room, unaware of the remorse in the deep blue eyes that followed her every movement.

CHAPTER SEVEN

MERRY'S tears had completely wet her pillow by the time she heard Gideon return to his cabin at just after one o'clock, sleep completely eluding her as she heard his movements next door.

She heard the final noise of the guests retiring for the night at about two o'clock, then she got noiselessly out of bed to dress and go up on deck, wearing a jumper that reached down to her thighs over her denims, as the evening was once again cool.

There was only the minimum of lighting on the deck now, and she stood at the stern of the yacht watching the wake they left behind them. The sea was a primitive force that made her shiver, dark and deep, and yet with a fascination that had called many a sailor to his death.

'Pagan, isn't it?'

She stiffened at the sound of that husky voice, aware of Gideon moving to stand at her side against the rail, the musky smell of his aftershave discernible to her in the sea-breeze. The sea might be pagan, but this man was more so, and like the sailors Merry couldn't escape the fascination.

'Couldn't you sleep?' He spoke again.

'No.' Still she didn't look at him.

'Neither could I,' he told her unnecessarily. 'You went to bed hours ago.' It was almost a question.

'I also slept this afternoon,' she reminded him abruptly.

'So you did.' He turned round to face the yacht, wearing a light blue sweat-shirt over navy denims, leaning back against the rail, suddenly closer to her as his arm brushed against hers. 'I'm sorry, Merry,' he said suddenly.

She turned to look at him, the sincerity of his words mirrored in the seriousness of his expression.

'I'm not doing a very good job of it, but I'm trying to handle the attraction between us in the best way possible for everyone concerned,' Gideon continued tautly. 'You came here to be with Anthea, to get to know her. I seem to have forgotten that in my own desire for you.'

'Gideon——'

'Please, let me finish,' he cut in harshly, seeming to speak almost to himself. 'I didn't expect, or want, to feel this way about you. I still don't. You're too young for me, the sort of girl that wants the "happy-ever-after".' He found it impossible to keep his scepticism out of his voice. 'Maybe if you weren't Anthea's daughter I would have tried to persuade you that my way is better. But you *are* her daughter, and that's a complication I can't handle. I deliberately goaded you tonight in the hope of making you angry with me. You're too much of a temptation when you cling to me and look up at me with those bewitching green eyes.'

She bit her lip, looking down at her hands. 'Please don't say any more.'

'No.' He pushed himself forcefully away from the railing. 'I'll see you in the morning, Merry.'

'Yes.' She continued to stare out into the darkness.

Moments later she felt hard hands on her shoulders, slowly turning her round, finding herself looking up into Gideon's tortured face. 'I can't do it,' he grated. 'I can't walk away from you! Will you be the one to walk away from me?' There was a note of pleading in his voice.

She shook her head. 'I can't do that either.'

'I don't how to behave with a girl like you, Merry, someone that's untouched,' he moaned. 'I told you, I've always preferred older women. There were no pretences with them——'

'Just sex.' She could see the indecision in his face, the uncertainty that was a totally alien emotion to this arrogant man, and she knew he told the truth, that he just didn't know how to handle his attraction to her. The fact that her mother was married to his father dictated that he behave differently with her, that he couldn't simply have the affair with her that he wanted to.

'Just sex,' he sighed. 'You know what it's like in the film business, Merry, even if you haven't been tainted with it yourself. I've been involved in it fifteen years now, and it's years since I met a girl who says no.'

It might have escaped Gideon's notice, but *he* was the one saying no; she hadn't said anything. And she still didn't.

'And that I've wanted to say no,' his eyes were hooded, 'but now I don't know what to do with you.'

She could see that, and she had no idea where they were going either. Maybe if Gideon could learn to love her in return—It was something that didn't even seem to have occurred to him! Maybe because, cynic that he was, he didn't believe in the emotion where he was concerned.

'Merry, for God's sake talk to me!' He shook her slightly.

'Kiss me,' she invited huskily.

His eyes widened. 'Kiss you . . .?'

'Don't tell me you don't know how,' she taunted, her gaze unwavering on his. If Gideon didn't believe in love then she would just have to make him.

'Oh, I know how, all right,' his mouth twisted, 'but

I've just finished explaining all the reasons why I shouldn't.'

'Coward!' she mocked him with his own taunt of earlier tonight. Gideon shook his head. 'Playing safe.'

'Didn't you once direct a film called *Living Dangerously*?' she asked with feigned innocence.

Gideon's breath caught in his throat. 'That was a different storyline completely.'

'So?' she challenged.

'Merry——' His words broke off as she took the initiative and moved into his arms, raising her lips to his in mute invitation. 'God, woman, you don't know how deep my desire for you goes!' he groaned.

'Show me,' she encouraged throatily, warmed by the fact that he had at last called her a woman.

He drew in a ragged breath, still not holding her in return. 'I daren't.'

Her eyes widened to mocking green pools. 'Daren't, Gideon . . .?'

His face darkened angrily. 'Don't goad me into something you'll later regret,' he rasped. 'You made it clear this morning that you couldn't accept an affair between us.'

'And you made it clear just now that you couldn't accept it either,' she nodded. 'Then what are we both still doing here?'

'Tempting the gods,' he moaned, his arms at last moving about her unwillingly, his hands lacing together at the base of her spine.

'Or each other,' Merry murmured huskily.

'Yes!' The word came out as an agonised groan, then Gideon's head bent to blot out the moonlight, parting her lips in deep surrender, murmuring low in his throat at her instantaneous response.

Merry arched into him, a small cry escaping her lips as he pulled her into the hardness of his body, the surging of his thighs leaving her in no doubt as to his desire for her, a deep throbbing desire that rocketed the senses. His lips devoured her, his hands roaming wildly over her body as he sought closer contact with her.

She could never have explained afterwards how it happened, she only knew the narrow width of a lounger suddenly held both of them as they lay turned into each other, Gideon's hands searching beneath the thickness of her dark jumper, his mouth exploring the lips that so enticed him.

Merry forgot everything but the pleasure she was giving and receiving, knowing Gideon was as affected by her caresses as deeply as she was by his, her hands caressing the thick muscles of his back and chest, the male nipples hardening beneath her touch.

Gideon froze as her hands moved down to the fastening of his denims, touching the flat tautness of his stomach there, sensing his hesitation at such intimacy. Finally his breath left him in a hiss, the tension left him as his weight pressed down on to her, crushing her hands between them, lifting himself up to allow her to once again caress his back, his own hands now probing the lacy cups of her bra, finding the single fastening before releasing the throbbing breasts into his waiting palms.

She gazed up at him in the darkness, her eyes dark pools of questioning green, begging him to make love to her.

He pushed the jumper up as it got in his way, capturing one fiery nipple between the hot furnace of his lips, moving to kiss the deep valley between her breasts before his tongue made love to her naval in a way that had her gasping her pleasure, then slowly moving up to capture the other aching nipple.

The molten fire his caresses induced flooded through her body, and this time when she caressed his thigh Gideon made no protest, his own hands exploring the warm softness of her own flesh beneath her unfastened denims, finding the warm pinnacle of her desire, his caresses driving her wild.

Suddenly he pinned her to the lounger, his body moving slowly against hers, their mouths meeting in a kiss that seemed to shoot them both up in flames, Merry's fingers entwining painfully in the dark thickness of his hair.

'This is ridiculous,' he suddenly groaned into her throat. 'We have two perfectly private cabins downstairs and we choose to make love here!'

She rained kisses along his jaw, his bare chest moulded to her breasts, causing pleasure with the rough scrape of the dark wiry hair that grew there. 'Then let's go to my cabin. We——' she broke off as she heard the sound of voices, knowing that Gideon had heard them too as he moved quickly to his feet, colour flooding her cheeks as she watched him fasten the clothing her willing fingers had so deftly undone. 'Gideon?' she whispered softly, looking up at him with love-drugged eyes.

He looked down at her impatiently. 'It's Anthea and my father,' he rasped. 'Anthea often has insomnia, especially this last year. Straighten your clothes, for God's sake!' he muttered. 'They could be here at any moment.'

Merry did so with shaking fingers, sitting up to push back her tangled hair, amazed at the composed expression on Gideon's face. If it weren't for the fact that his body still betrayed his arousal no one would have guessed at their heated caresses of a few minutes ago.

Gideon pulled her roughly to her feet, pushing her down the steps on the opposite side of the deck to his father and stepmother, the two of them disappearing below deck without being seen.

The rigidness of Gideon's expression reminded Merry of the first night they had met, and she knew he was angry. Whether with himself or her she didn't know.

They parted at her cabin door, where Gideon left her after staring down at her with compelling eyes for several long, silent minutes.

'Gideon!' she stopped him as he would have entered his own cabin without having spoken a word to her.

He shook his head, pale beneath his tan. 'I can't do it, Merry, I can't take your innocence from you,' he rasped softly. 'You're Anthea's daughter, and that makes you something special, something I can't despoil with an affair. This should never have started between us—although with the close confines, and the supposed intimacy of our relationship, perhaps it was inevitable,' he sighed.

Merry felt pain shoot through her body. 'You think that's all it is?' she choked.

'Of course,' he nodded distantly. 'Once we get off the yacht and return to our own life, our own friends, we'll laugh at this attraction between us. After all,' he gave a derisive laugh, 'you're my sister, damn it!'

Merry gave a mumbled goodnight, wondering if she would ever laugh again, and went into her cabin. So much for hoping Gideon would come to love her! He believed it was only this close confinement that had caused the attraction in the first place!

But she didn't. She could accept that her antagonism from their first meeting had been because of an instantaneous attraction to him on her part. She wasn't usually so aggressively outspoken to a complete stranger, and she had surprised herself that time. But loving Gideon wasn't something she had wanted or expected, and it didn't look as if he was capable of loving her in return.

She was woken the next morning with an abrupt knock on the cabin door, and forced her eyes open, a glance at the clock telling her it was after ten o'clock.

'Come in!' she called, expecting the stewardess who brought her morning cup of coffee, and the colour left her face as Gideon walked in.

The gaze that swept over her was completely impersonal. 'You aren't feeling ill again?' he bit out curtly.

Merry blushed. 'No, I just—I didn't sleep well.' And he knew why, knew that she couldn't possibly have slept after the way they had parted last night. Gideon seemed to have had no such difficulty, looking as fresh and alert as usual.

He nodded. 'Niko tells me you wrote some postcards yesterday.'

Merry frowned. 'Yes?'

'If you give them to me I'll post them for you.'

Her eyes widened. 'We've stopped again?' It didn't feel as if they had, the yacht was gently swaying.

'At Mykonos,' Gideon confirmed. 'I'm just going ashore now. Mykonos doesn't have a very big harbour, so we've thrown down anchor in the bay. Some of us are going ashore.'

Did that mean Linda too? No doubt it did. Merry bit back her jealousy with an effort. She didn't have any right to be jealous; Gideon had made that only too clear.

She got out of bed, knowing the silky pyjamas she wore were adequate covering. Gideon had certainly seen her in less! The postcards were in the bottom of her spacious handbag, and it took her several minutes to find them, all the time conscious of Gideon's gaze burning a hole in her back. Finally she turned triumphantly with the postcards, to surprise a look on Gideon's face that she didn't understand, an expression that he quickly masked as he snatched the postcards out of her hand and turned to leave.

'Have a nice day,' she said softly.

He turned abruptly. 'Thanks. Don't get sunburnt,' he rasped, and closed the door hard behind him.

Much he would care if she burnt to a crisp, Merry thought angrily. Damn him! Damn him to hell! Falling in love was supposed to be the most beautiful thing ever to happen in your life, not to make you feel like crying all the time.

But crying was what she most felt like, and she gave in to the emotion, and was still crying into her pillow when she heard the door open behind her.

'I did knock, but—My dear!' Anthea Steele's concerned voice interrupted her sobs as the other woman came to sit on the side of the bed. 'Merry, what is it?' she asked gently. 'Would you like me to get Gideon for you?' she said as Merry continued to cry. 'I don't think he's gone ashore yet, and——'

'No!' Merry turned with a tear-stained face. 'Don't you dare stop him going into Mykonos—I wouldn't want him to miss one moment of pleasure!'

Anthea held back a smile at the angry words. 'He thought your trip out yesterday might have tired you,' she soothed softly.

Merry's eyes flashed deeply green. 'He left me to rest all yesterday afternoon. I'm not senile!'

'But you have been ill.'

'Only one night,' she snapped.

Anthea couldn't hold back her smile any longer. 'If it's any consolation, Gideon is scowling at everyone too.'

'He—he is?' She wiped her cheeks with the back of her hand.

'Yes.' Anthea handed her a tissue from her bag. 'You two certainly seem to strike sparks off each other! It's a long time since I've seen Gideon so incensed.'

'Angry, you mean,' Merry sniffed inelegantly.

'Very,' the other woman chuckled. 'Over the years Gideon has become very cynical, even blasé, about life and the people he meets. You've certainly shaken him out of his complacency.'

'You don't seem to mind,' Merry frowned.

'I welcome it.' Anthea watched as she got up to collect her clothes together for the day, moving to sit on the chair as Meredith straightened the bed. 'And so does his father. Samuel has been worried about Gideon for some time now. Do you love Gideon?' she asked softly.

Merry blushed fiery red, shaken by the bluntness of the question. 'I—I——'

'Don't answer,' Anthea sighed. 'I should never have asked.'

She longed to talk to someone about her feelings for Gideon, and who better than her own mother? But she didn't have that closeness to Anthea, and despite coming to like the other woman she wasn't sure if they would ever be able to achieve the closeness of a mother and daughter.

Anthea stood up as she saw her hesitation. 'I'll leave you to get dressed. Come up and join us on deck when you're ready.'

Merry's eyes widened. 'You aren't going ashore with the others?'

'I've seen enough Greek islands this last month to last me a lifetime,' the other woman derided. 'I'm just going to rest today.'

Anthea did look tired, the shadows were back in her eyes, and Merry was reminded that she had had a breakdown not so long ago. Mainly because of her.

'I'll come up on deck soon,' she told her softly,

realising that today would be the perfect time to get to know this woman who had become a mother while still a child herself.

She showered and dressed once Anthea had left, putting on white shorts and a green sun-top, brushing her hair loose about her shoulders, leaving her face bare of make-up.

The loungers on deck seemed to be mainly occupied when she stepped up into the blazing sunshine; the sky was a deep cloudless blue, reflecting in the deep, deep blue sea. She leant over the rail, gazing at the beauty that was Mykonos, the beautiful glistening white houses nestled in the red earthy hills, the sea lapping against the golden sand. Several people were swimming in the warm water. Merry strained her eyes to see if Gideon were one of them, but the yacht was really too far away from the shore for her to tell if he were on the beach or not.

'Do you—My God!' Samuel Steele rasped as Merry turned to look at him, frowning when she saw how pale he had gone. 'I—I'm sorry,' he shook his head dazedly. 'For a moment you reminded me of—of someone else.' He forced a smile. 'I was going to ask if you regretted not going ashore with Gideon. Mykonos is very lovely.'

Her heart contracted with apprehension, knowing Anthea was the 'someone else' she reminded him of. It was inevitable that, like Gideon, this man who loved Anthea so much should eventually see the similarity. How long before he realised the truth?

'He didn't ask me to go with him,' she answered his question, her voice husky.

'No?' he smiled. 'You'll have to forgive my son. What little manners I managed to instil in him before he got too old to ignore every word I say seem to be forgotten the moment he's with you. I'm pleased to say you give as good as you get.'

Merry's mouth quirked mischievously, the sun hot on her arms and throat. 'Are fathers supposed to be pleased about that?'.

'If their sons are as arrogant as Gideon, yes,' he grinned. 'It's about time someone stood up to him.'

'Gideon doesn't feel the same way.'

Samuel patted her hand as it rested on the rail. 'If you'll forgive my saying so, my dear, Gideon doesn't always know what's good for him.' He shook his head. 'He's had too many yes-women in his life.'

A delicate blush darkened her cheeks. 'What makes you think I haven't said yes too?'

Samuel's smile deepened. 'If you had Gideon wouldn't be in this foul temper all the time.'

Merry turned away, her expression bitter. 'You might be surprised, Mr Steele,' she sighed, knowing that last night she had definitely said yes—and Gideon had turned her down.

Samuel's gaze levelled on her pained expression. 'I'm sorry, my dear,' he said softly. 'I seem to have delved into something very private between you and Gideon. I hope you'll forgive me?'

'Of course,' she forced a bright smile to her lips. 'Where's Mrs Steele? I told her I would join her.'

His smile became indulgent at the mention of his wife. 'Anthea has fallen asleep,' he nodded towards one of the loungers situated in the shaded area, where Anthea was looking beautiful even in sleep. 'I'm afraid she doesn't sleep too well at night. We walked on deck for several hours last night.'

Of course they had—hadn't it been their timely interruption that brought an end to Gideon making love to her! Heavens, Gideon was so much on her mind that she found it impossible to think of anything else! Well, she wouldn't think of him today, she would make it out of sight, out of mind.

'I'm sorry,' she said with genuine sympathy for the other woman's insomnia. 'Are we close enough to shore for me to swim over the side?' she asked hopefully.

Samuel frowned. 'I suppose so,' he considered. 'Although if you want to swim I can always get someone to take you ashore?'

'No! Er—no,' she answered more calmly. 'I thought I could just go in over the side here. If that's all right?'

'I don't see why not,' he shrugged. 'If that's what you would like?'

'I would,' she nodded.

'I'll make the arrangements——'

'If it's any bother——'

'Not at all, Merry,' he dismissed with an arrogance that more than equalled his son's, and strode off.

It didn't take her long to strip down to her bikini, and it seemed that the ladder was still lowered from where Gideon had gone ashore.

The water was cold and invigorating as she dived neatly off the side, making her gasp with the surprise of it. But once the shock had worn off she found she was enjoying herself; the water was quite warm, and beautifully clear.

'Can I join you, mermaid?'

She looked up to find Michael Woods poised on the side of the yacht, his only clothing a pair of black swimming trunks, his lithe body deeply tanned.

Merry smiled at him. 'Please do.'

There was the faintest ripple as Michael dived into the water a few feet away from her, surfacing to shake the water from his hair and face, his eyes alight with mischief. 'I could hardly believe my eyes when I looked over the side and saw a mermaid,' he grinned as he swam easily to her side.

'Shouldn't you be a little more romantic in Greece?' she taunted as she trod water beside him.

He grimaced. 'Probably. How about Aphrodite?'

'That will do,' she laughed. 'And I suppose you're Apollo?'

'I leave that privilege to Gideon,' he taunted. 'I don't have the body for it.'

Her smile faded at the mention of Gidion. And Michael was right, he wasn't as powerfully built or as muscled as Gideon. She turned to swim off a little way. 'Where's Linda?' she asked.

'Mykonos.' Michael's smooth strokes easily kept him at her side.

Her body stiffened in the water. 'Mykonos . . .?'

'Mm. She decided to keep Gideon company.'

'They've gone alone?' She tried to make her tone sound casual.

'Yes,' Michael confirmed heavily, showing he was no more enamoured with the situation than she was.

So 'some of us' really meant Linda and Gideon! No wonder he hadn't invited her along; she would have cramped his style today too. But how could he do that to poor Michael? Quite easily, she answered herself, especially as Linda seemed more than willing to encourage him.

'Oh well, there's always me,' she told Michael brightly.

He shook his head. 'I don't think so. You belong to Gideon. Besides, I love Linda,' he revealed sadly.

'And I——'

'Yes?' he prompted softly.

She blushed. 'I care about Gideon,' she amended. 'But it would teach them both a lesson if they came back and found we haven't missed them as much as we should have done.'

'Aphrodite, you wouldn't be suggesting we do a little flirting of our own?' he teased.

Merry looked at him in challenge, knowing from

Linda's reaction when she had suggested 'cultivating' Michael that she wouldn't appreciate her spending the day with him now. Maybe a little jealousy was what the other woman needed.

'I'm suggesting we spend the day together,' she shrugged. 'Nothing more—and nothing less,' she added softly.

Michael chuckled his enjoyment. 'Aphrodite, I'm starting to feel sorry for Gideon! He doesn't know yet what he's taken on,' he explained at her questioning look.

'A hellion, he called me,' she told him dryly.

'At least that,' Michael nodded. 'Okay, I'm game, Aphrodite. But don't blame me if Gideon explodes. He seems to watch over you like some damned guard-dog. That night I came to see you when you were sick——'

'Don't remind me!' she groaned.

'He took care of you admirably, something I wouldn't have believed him capable of.'

Merry frowned. 'You make him sound very selfish.'

He shook his head. 'Not selfish exactly, just someone who knows what he wants and how to get it with the minimum of effort. I know him well enough to realise he won't like my being with you. The night you were ill he watched my every move.'

Merry grimaced. 'I was hardly at my most attractive!'

Michael grinned. 'Anything that had looked like a sexual move on my part would have got me a black eye. Thank goodness, *I* don't happen to be at the peak of my libido that time of the morning, especially when I've been dragged from my warm, comfortable bed. But Gideon watched me like a hawk.'

'That's because——'

'Yes?' He watched her with narrowed eyes.

She evaded his glance, biting her bottom lip. She had almost revealed that Gideon was so protective because he regarded her as his stepsister. 'He's just protective,' she mumbled.

'Where you're concerned, yes. If it weren't for the fact that I happen to be Anthea's doctor I think he would have had me thrown off by now,' Michael said ruefully.

'I'm sure you're exaggerating,' she blushed.

'No,' he said firmly.

She shrugged. 'Are we here to swim or talk? I'm starting to get cold,' she added pointedly.

'Then let's swim.' He took her hint.

They spent a lighthearted day together, having lunch with Anthea and Samuel, although Merry felt sure that both of them spent the better part of the day watching for the return of Gideon and Linda. The other couple seemed in no hurry to come back to the yacht, and it was late afternoon when Merry spotted the launch returning from shore. She had been leaning over the side, a bored expression on her face, but now she turned and walked slowly back to Michael's side, sitting down in the chair next to him beneath the umbrella shade.

He looked up from the book he had been reading, putting it down at the angry set of her mouth. 'They're coming back,' he guessed.

'Yes,' she bit out. 'After six hours they've finally decided to return.' Her eyes flashed as she looked at him. 'If you have any sense you'll beat Linda.'

Michael spluttered with laughter. 'I can't see her accepting that.'

'You aren't going to ask her permission, for goodness' sake!' Merry exclaimed heatedly. 'Just put her over your knee and beat her.'

He still smiled. 'You're very physical.'

She gave a rueful smile. 'Only because I would like to punch Gideon on the nose. I doubt I'd be able to reach,' she derided her height, all the time conscious that the launch was back now, and Gideon and Linda were on board, walking down the deck towards them.

'I'll lift you,' Michael promised dryly.

The thought of that made such an amusing picture that Merry couldn't help her splutter of laughter. She was pleased about her genuine humour as she felt the shadow pass over her, knowing Gideon was standing beside her chair, sensing him there even as she caught the faint smell of his spicy aftershave, the smile still on her lips as she glanced up at him. If looks could have frozen she would have been turned to a block of ice in that moment!

Linda clung to Gideon's arm, her eyes hard as she took in the intimacy of the situation between Merry and Michael. 'It doesn't look as if we've been missed, darling,' she drawled to Gideon.

He made no reply, and Michael didn't seem inclined to deny the reply, so it was left to Merry to make some effort at conversation. 'Did you have a nice day?' Her smile didn't waver.

'Not as good as you, apparently,' the other woman said hardly.

Merry lightly touched Michael's hand as it rested on the table in front of them. 'Oh, we've had a lovely time, haven't we?' she smiled at him.

'Yes.' He took his cue from her, and did not elaborate.

Linda looked incensed at the way Merry was touching *her* fiancé's hand, and Merry had an idea it would be a long time before the other woman treated Michael so casually again. 'If you wouldn't mind, Michael,' Linda said hardly, her eyes snapping with anger, 'I would like to talk to you. Alone.'

'Oh, don't mind us,' Merry said lightly. 'Gideon and I have a lot to talk about ourselves. Don't we, darling?' She looked at him in challenge.

He made no reply, but pulled her to her feet to push her in the direction of the lower deck and made straight for her cabin, pushing her roughly inside once she had unlocked the door.

'I warned you!' he ground out darkly. 'I warned you to stay away from Michael.'

She gave a nonchalant shrug. 'You were with Linda. I didn't have much choice.'

His eyes narrowed. 'Do you mean he forced you to spend the day with him?'

Merry smiled, seeing the anger flare higher in his eyes. And she enjoyed seeing it! Just who did he think he was, disappearing for most of the day with another woman and then accusing *her*! 'Don't be ridiculous, Gideon,' she mocked him. 'I enjoyed being with him, actually. And you had stolen his fiancée,' she got in her dig at him.

He scowled down at her. 'Linda invited herself along. I just had to get off the yacht. And you know why, don't you?' he rasped.

Her eyes widened. 'Why?'

'For God's sake!' he snapped. 'Because of last night!'

'Last night?' Merry feigned puzzlement. 'Oh, that,' she taunted with a smile. 'But you said we would come to laugh at last night.'

'Not yet, damn you!' he ground out, his eyes glittering. 'How can you treat it so casually, Merry?'

'I'm your sister, remember?' she mocked. 'And we're going to forget last night ever happened.'

She had pushed him too far with her dig about being his sister, and his fingers dug painfully into her arms as he dragged her against him, kissing her with a roughness that wasn't meant to be enjoyed, on any level.

Her eyes glistened with unshed tears as he broke the kiss, her head bent back as she looked at him defiantly.

'Only you wouldn't kiss a sister like that, would you, Gideon?' she choked. 'Would you?' she prompted hardly as his fingers tightened convulsively on her arms.

He thrust her away from him and turned away. 'Stay away from me, Meredith. Just stay away from me!' He slammed out of the cabin.

CHAPTER EIGHT

MERRY had never been so unhappy in her life, although to anyone observing her she looked like any young girl would enjoying her cruise, sunbathing most of the day, spending the evenings dancing or simply listening to music. And always with Gideon, which was where the problems arose.

As far as everyone else on the yacht was concerned she and Gideon were closer than ever, spending all of their time together on the five days sailing to Spain. Gideon insisted she be with him every minute of the day, and as Linda had suddenly seemed to develop a deep jealousy where Michael was concerned—much to his delight!—that wasn't too difficult to achieve.

And Merry hated it! She hated his falsely solicitous manner, his arrogant taking of kisses whenever they were with other people. And most of all she hated his coldness when they were alone, the way he virtually ignored her existence.

Several times she managed to escape him and spend time with Anthea, finding the two of them were building up an affection in spite of themselves. Merry liked the other woman, was coming to care for her gentleness, her giving nature, and far from disapproving of her as Gideon's girl-friend, as he had said she would at the start of the cruise, Anthea actually seemed to encourage the relationship.

'She thinks we're genuinely in love,' Gideon derided on the eve of their arrival in Cadiz, their last port of call before returning to England.

The two of them were sitting alone in a corner of the lounge, where several couples were dancing, the soft music adding to the intimacy of the evening, another evening when Gideon had somehow managed to ensure their privacy from interruption. He was obviously reluctant to have to act the loving boy-friend too often, his arm about her bare shoulders being sufficient claim to a relationship between them when they were alone like this.

Merry had come to know this man during the last five days, to know his charm, his wit, and lastly his coldness. And she loved him more than ever, though she knew only pain at his derision of the emotion.

'She actually approves of you as a wife for me,' he added harshly, taking a large swallow of his whisky, the dimmed lighting making his hair appear almost black, the white cocktail jacket tailored to his broad shoulders and narrow waist.

'I thought she was supposed to like me,' Merry said shakily.

'Not as a wife for me!'

She turned away to shield the hurt she felt at his utter rejection of her emotionally. She had harboured no illusions or hopes of Gideon coming to care for her, she knew his views of love and marriage with regard to himself, and had learnt only too well the truth of Linda's words. Gideon would never settle down with one woman, would never marry. He had been restless with her this last week and a half, obviously longing to get back to 'his own life, his own friends', felt restricted by this apparent single-minded attraction to her.

'I'm sorry,' she mumbled. 'Maybe we should just tell Anthea the truth.'

'Are you ready to accept that?' he rasped.

She swallowed hard. 'I—I like her——'

'Enough to be her daughter?'

She flushed. 'I think so.'

'It's no good *thinking* it, Merry,' he scorned harshly. 'You have to be sure. You've seen Anthea, she couldn't take losing you once she'd found you.'

Her eyes flashed, the same deep green as the clinging dress she wore, with her long hair loose about her shoulders, the middle parting feathered away from her face. 'All parents have to let their children go eventually,' she snapped. 'My father has already done so, although our emotional ties remain as strong as ever.'

She wasn't stupid, she knew that Anthea's friendly manner hid a fragile emotional stability, that the other woman did indeed live on her nerves as Gideon had first implied. And she wasn't going to jeopardise that stability; she resented Gideon for thinking she was.

'That's all Anthea will want too,' he told her coldly. 'But I think you should put off telling her who you are until you're sure you can be what she needs.'

Merry sighed. 'I was thinking of you. Once she knows the truth you'll be free of this pretence.'

His mouth twisted. 'I think I can take another three days of it.'

She wasn't sure she could! It was hell having to respond to his warmth in public but knowing only his coldness when they were alone. That he intended no more relapses of the kind they had shared on deck that night was obvious, and if he still felt attracted to her he hid it well. Too well!

'Could I have this dance, Merry?'

She looked up to find Samuel Steele standing in front

of her, and she nodded her acceptance as she went willingly into his waiting arms. She had spoken several times with Gideon's father the last few days, found him an intelligent and charming man. Rather like his son! She found the similarity between the two men very disturbing.

'*Who* are you, Merry?'

She blinked up at Samuel Steele, surprised by the question. 'I'm sorry?' she frowned her puzzlement.

'Would you mind if we went outside for a while?' he suggested gravely. 'I'd like to talk to you.'

'Er—Of course.' Her puzzlement was obvious as she allowed him to guide her out into the clear moonlit night, conscious that Gideon watched them with narrowed eyes.

Samuel led her to a quiet part of the deck, sitting her down in one of the armchairs before seating himself in front of her, effectively blocking her from view of anyone curious enough to look their way. Merry felt uneasy at the grim look in his eyes, and the soft music filtering from the lounge did nothing to soothe her nerves.

'I repeat,' Samuel said slowly, 'who are you, Merry? And I want the truth, not this game of charades you and Gideon have been playing this last week or so.'

She moistened her lips nervously with the tip of her tongue, not prepared for this at all. 'I'm Meredith Charles,' she answered evasively. 'Gideon and I are—friends.'

'So you keep telling everyone,' Samuel derided. 'And I don't doubt that there's an attraction between you, maybe even more than that. But I've been watching you, surely you've been aware of that?'

Yes, she had been aware of it, but she had put it down to mere curiosity about his son's relationship with a young girl who seemed to anger him more than she attracted him. But it seemed she had been wrong, that Samuel Steele had seen much more than that.

'I didn't mean to, but just now I overheard part of your conversation with Gideon.' He watched as the colour slowly drained from her cheeks. 'So,' he sighed, her guilt feelings obvious for him to see, 'who are you? And what do you have to do with Anthea?'

She could hear his concern for his wife. 'You must know that Gideon would never hurt Anthea——'

'I *thought* he wouldn't, but now I'm beginning to wonder,' he frowned darkly.

'Oh, please don't,' Merry pleaded. 'He has only thought of your wife from the start.'

'The start of what?'

'I—I really don't know how to explain.' She bit her lip.

'Maybe the beginning would be a good idea,' he prompted softly.

She sighed. 'I don't really know much about the beginning.' She looked up at him unflinchingly. 'You see, I was only a baby,' her voice was husky. 'And Anthea was just seventeen years old.'

There was a convulsive movement in Samuel's throat, a choked sound as his avid gaze searched her features with disbelieving eyes, the colour slowly ebbing from his cheeks. 'Dear God,' he choked. 'I should have known, should have realised . . .! Every time I looked at you I knew you reminded me of someone. So Gideon actually found you. He found you!'

'Yes,' she confirmed huskily.

Samuel looked as if he were about to collapse, there was a greyness to his face. 'How did he do it?' He seemed to speak almost to himself. 'I looked for you myself,' he shook his head. 'And every time I came up against some bureaucrat who told me the parents of an adopted child have no rights.'

Merry smiled without humour. 'Gideon doesn't have your scruples, Mr Steele,' she said gently. 'He certainly doesn't let things like bureaucracy stand in his way.'

'In other words, he broke all the rules,' Samuel said with a return of his own arrogance.

'Yes,' this time her smile did contain real humour. 'Gideon is a man who makes up his own rules—and breaks them too if they conflict with what he wants.'

'You know my son very well,' he said dryly.

'I've tried to.'

'It isn't always easy,' he agreed ruefully. 'I'm still trying to work out the reason for the pretence of being his girl-friend,' he frowned.

'That was my fault, I'm afraid,' Merry admitted. 'I wasn't exactly overjoyed to learn I had a mother I didn't even know about.' She explained not knowing of her adoption, seeing Samuel's expression soften with understanding. 'I'm afraid I wasn't very co-operative about meeting Anthea.'

'But as usual my son wasn't taking no for an answer.'

'Actually, he did,' she said with some surprise. After coming to know Gideon the last ten days she had also come to know that he could be very adept at getting his own way. 'Then he came up with this idea once I'd agreed to the meeting. It seemed to be the solution to everything, getting to know Anthea without her knowing who I was.'

'And what have you decided?' Samuel probed intently.

'I——'

'She hasn't decided anything yet, Dad,' a harsh voice rasped out of the darkness behind them. 'And she isn't going to be pressurised into making that decision by you or anyone else!' Gideon stepped forward into the light, his face livid with fury. 'I thought we'd just agreed that who you were was still to be kept between the two of us.' His eyes were accusing as he spoke to Merry.

She bit her lip at this open anger. 'I——'

'Merry didn't tell me,' Samuel answered his son, and stood up, as tall as the younger man, if not as powerfully built. He certainly wasn't daunted by Gideon as other men were. 'At least, not until I half guessed it.'

Gideon drew in a deep controlling breath, his hands thrust into the pockets of his trousers. 'And how did you do that?' he derided harshly.

His father shrugged. 'It wasn't too difficult. Merry is very like Anthea.'

She felt relieved at the older man's defence of her, knowing that he only told half the truth. Maybe in time, with his suspicions already aroused, he might have realised her connection to Anthea, but he certainly would never have guessed it here and now. But she needed defending against Gideon's anger, and she didn't feel capable of doing it herself; she felt drained by her conversation with Samuel Steele.

'Yes, she is,' Gideon rasped tightly.

'Anthea should be told——'

'No!' his son bit out determinedly.

His father and Merry both looked at him in surprise, Merry more so than the older man. Gideon had been adament in the beginning that his stepmother be told the truth. What had changed his mind? Could it be that he wanted her so far out of his life he was hoping she would decide not to tell Anthea she was her daughter? It seemed to be the only explanation, and it was one that hurt her unbearably.

Not that it showed as she met the challenge in his gaze. 'I think the time has come for her to be told.'

'And I said no!' He moved forward ominously.

'Gideon——'

'Stay out of this, Dad,' Gideon ground out. 'I've been handling this so far——'

'Not very well, if you want my opinion,' his father flared.

'I don't,' Gideon snapped. 'And——'

'Please!' Merry gasped her dismay, shocked at the antipathy that had roared up between father and son, seeing the two of them glaring fiercely at each other. 'Please don't argue about it.' She touched Gideon's arm tentatively, quickly removing her hand as he looked down at her, his jaw rigid, a pulse beating erratically in his tautly held neck.

'Is everything all right, darling?' Anthea joined them, slipping her hand in the crook of her husband's arm. 'You're all looking very tense.' She looked at them enquiringly, her brows raised.

A curious stillness settled over the other three, Merry looking anxiously from father to son, seeing the challenge in each of their faces as they waited for the other to speak. Neither looked as if they intended backing down, both had a determined set to their mouth.

Merry could have cried with frustration, looking at her mother, who was looking deeply puzzled. She couldn't bear for the other woman to be told the truth about her in these circumstances. Couldn't Gideon and Samuel see that? Or was their anger with each other more important than Anthea's health?

'Darling?' Anthea prompted.

At that moment Samuel seemed to become aware of Merry's dismayed expression, and collected himself with effort, turning to smile down at his wife. 'Of course everything is all right. Gideon and I were just have a slight—disagreement about what time we would reach Cadiz tomorrow.'

Merry felt the breath leave her body in a relieved sigh, sensing Gideon's tension lessening too.

Anthea's frown still remained. 'Why don't you just ask the Captain?'

Samuel smiled. 'Don't be so practical, darling,' he teased. 'You know Gideon and I enjoy a little argument now and then.'

'As long as it *is* only a little one,' she accepted uncertainly.

'Of course,' her husband chided softly.

'If you say so,' Anthea shrugged. 'Although I still think it would have been easier to ask the Captain.'

'Darling, you know I . . .' Samuel's voice faded as he and Anthea strolled back to the lounge.

Merry's arm was grasped painfully. 'You little fool!' Gideon muttered into her ear. 'You should have just played dumb when my father questioned you. Why the hell did you tell him who you are?' he rasped, his eyes glittering furiously.

She refused to be cowed by his anger, to even acknowledge the fact that his fingers were bruising her arm. 'He asked me,' she told him simply.

His mouth tightened. 'You aren't usually that forthcoming.'

'It depends who's asking the questions.'

'You little——'

'Yes?' she queried calmly as he broke off.

'Never mind,' he dismissed harshly. 'Just let things ride with Anthea for now. There's plenty of time to tell her.'

'Only three days,' she pointed out.

'Then wait that amount of time,' he snapped impatiently. 'God damn it, what's your hurry all of a sudden? Hell, it——'

'When you've quite finished swearing at me?' Merry said coldly, her brows arched over cool green eyes, the gentle breeze ruffling the darkness of her hair.

'I haven't even started yet,' he bit out.

'I—We're being watched.' She turned away, seeing several other couples strolling on deck too now. This might be large as yachts go—she really had no comparisons to make!—but it still afforded its occupants little privacy. At this moment she would like to tell Gideon exactly what she thought of him, but as that was impossible to do she satisfied herself with just glaring at him.

'I couldn't give a damn about that,' he ignored the other couples.

'But I could!' she snapped softly.

'Oh, to hell with this!' He released her abruptly. 'I'm going to bed.'

Merry blinked dazedly; this the last thing she had been expecting. 'But it's only ten-thirty!'

'So?' His mouth twisted, his eyes narrowed. 'Is there some rule that says I can't go to bed at that time?'

'No——'

'Believe me, I've done it often enough in the past.' He raised one dark brow suggestively.

Colour darkened her cheeks. 'I'll say goodnight, then,' she said stiffly, knowing that his early nights in the past hadn't been spent alone.

'Oh, I doubt it will be that,' he mocked dryly. 'Do you want to go into Cadiz tomorrow?' he asked abruptly.

'I—Yes, I think so.' She was taken aback by his change of mood; the tormentor had gone now. 'I've enjoyed the relaxation of the sail from Mykonos, but I think I'd like to get on to firm ground for a while.'

Gideon frowned. 'Still feeling seasick?'

'Just the odd twinge,' she shrugged. 'Nothing to worry about.'

He nodded. 'I'll take you shopping in Cadiz tomorrow. Unless you would like to go to the bullring?' he quirked a mocking eyebrow.

'No, thank you,' she shuddered. 'It's so cruel!'

'It's an honourable death.'

'Honourable!' she repeated disgustedly. 'It's barbaric!'

'So is the fox-hunt in England.'

'I don't approve of that either,' she snapped.

Gideon began to smile. 'I didn't think you would. You're a gentle little thing under all that fire and brimstone, aren't you.'

'I think that may be a backhanded compliment!' Merry grimaced.

He began to chuckle. 'Probably. I'll see you in the morning.' He moved away.

'Gideon?' she waited for him to slowly turn, 'what time *will* we arrive in Cadiz tomorrow?'

He shrugged. 'I haven't the faintest idea. Why don't you ask the Captain?' he derided, walking down the stairs that led to the berth deck.

And with that last taunt Merry decided she might as well go to bed too. It had been quite an evening! But at least Samuel Steele knew the truth now, maybe he could persuade Gideon that it would be best for all of them if Anthea were also told the truth. Although she wouldn't count on it!

Cadiz was a bustling port, Merry discovered when they had docked early next morning, where barrels of brandy and sherry from the vineyards in Jerez were being carefully and methodically loaded aboard the transport vessels.

'Like to see where it's produced?' Gideon had joined her on deck without her being aware of it. 'I might even let you try a few of the sherries—as long as you promise not to get drunk. You're difficult enough to handle sober, let alone drunk!'

Gideon's early night certainly seemed to have agreed

with him, his humour was more biting than usual this morning. 'I don't happen to like brandy or sherry,' she told him haughtily. 'And I'd like to buy some presents, for my father and friends.'

'Okay,' he shrugged, very dark and attractive in a cream shirt and cream fitted trousers. 'I'm willing to play tourist if you are.'

'I *am* a tourist,' she snapped, striding over to help herself to breakfast.

'A little touchy today, aren't we?' Gideon spoke softly against her earlobe, his lips touching her skin, his warm breath stirring her hair.

She turned to glare at him. 'Do I have anything to feel happy about?'

'I would have thought so. There's the sun, the excitement of a new country—and me,' he popped a button mushroom in her mouth as she went to protest at his presence making her feel happy, 'as your personal guide. A lot of women could ask for nothing more,' he put another tiny mushroom into her mouth as she would once more have answered him, 'could they?' His face was only inches from her own.

She emptied her mouth of the mushrooms and swallowed hard. 'A lot of women probably don't know how moody you are.'

'Moody? Me?' Gideon somehow managed to look hurt. 'I'm the most even-tempered of men.'

'Hah!' she showed her disgust. 'And I don't like mushrooms,' she warned as he would have put another one in her mouth.

'Liar.' He popped it between her slightly parted lips, somehow managing to caress her lips in the process. 'I've watched every morning as you piled them on to your plate.'

'Why, you——'

'Naughty,' he tapped her lightly on the nose,

continuing to flirt with her. 'Let's not ruin the day, Merry,' he was suddenly serious, 'it's our last one in port.'

Now she knew the reason for his good humour! It was the last day he would have to spend entertaining her, once they were sailing again he could go back to making sure they were always alone, when his manner would be cold and distant. Her own mood plummetted.

They turned left out of the harbour once they had left the yacht, crossing the road to enter the network of tiny streets that contained a series of shops that sold everything, from the fans and beautiful shawls Spain was known for, to Cartier jewellery. It was to the latter that Gideon led her, watching her face as she gazed in awe at all the exquisite jewellery.

'For a woman who doesn't like jewellery ...' he drawled mockingly.

She gave him an irritated glance, then turned to continue walking. 'I didn't say I don't like it. I just refused to accept any from you.'

'It isn't unheard-of for a brother to buy his sister presents.' He stayed at her side.

Merry knew he was mocking her with her own taunts, and she walked off moodily. The only thing that had seemed to penetrate his cold mask the last few days had been her taunts about being his sister, now he had used it very effectively to upset her! She didn't feel like his sister, she didn't *want* to be his sister, she just wanted him to notice her.

Gideon walked beside her as if nothing had happened, his stride relaxed and at ease. 'I bought them for you, you know,' he told her softly.

'Really?' she said distantly.

'Really,' he nodded. 'On the morning we left England.'

'I still don't want them. What would I do with jewellery like that?' She could only guess at its worth!

'Wear it,' he mocked dryly.

She turned to him angrily. 'Look, Gideon, maybe the women who usually flit in and out of your life expect and like expensive presents from you, but I'm not one of them. Keep the jewellery for your next—woman,' she added scornfully. 'I don't need it.' She already loved him enough without receiving presents from him!

'No, you look, Merry,' he swung her round roughly, uncaring that people were staring at them. 'I've tried to be nice to you today. I've gone out of my way to——'

'To what?' she stormed, her eyes blazing. 'Don't do me any favours, Gideon. If there's somewhere else you would rather be then damn well go there! I don't need——'

'Don't say you don't need me!' he shook her hard. 'I don't need you either, but I'm stuck with you.'

'And I with you, until *you* decide we can all end this farce!' She shook off his grasp, and the rest of their shopping was done in silence, Merry ignoring Gideon as she bought presents for her father and Vanda, only acknowledging his presence again when he suggested they stop at one of the outside cafés to have a drink in the heat of the day.

She made no effort at conversation with him as they drank their coffee, acknowledging with a wave some of the other guests from the yacht as they too wandered about the narrow streets browsing in the shops.

Gideon gave every indication of being unconcerned by her silence, sipping at his coffee with obvious enjoyment, the dark sunglasses shielding the expression in his eyes, reminding Merry of the first time she had seen him. They had come a long way since then! But Gideon didn't seem to like her any better—and she loved him.

'Can we join you?'

She looked up to see Anthea and Samuel had

approached their table without her being aware of it, her thoughts deeply on Gideon. She smiled. 'Of course. We——' but before she could say any more Anthea gave a startled gasp and slid gracefully to the ground.

Gideon and Samuel moved simultaneously, going down on their knees beside the unconscious woman.

Samuel had gone grey. 'Anthea? Anthea!' He sounded frantic, gently tapping her hand.

'What the hell good is shouting at her going to do?' Gideon rasped, looking just as anxious.

Merry pushed them both out of the way. 'And what good is the two of you shouting at each other going to do her either?' She glared at them both. 'Get her up off the ground and into a chair. She's probably hurting her leg lying like that.' One of Anthea's legs were bent up beneath her, and couldn't possibly be comfortable. 'Well, come on,' she encouraged both men as they seemed to be made of stone.

Samuel managed to lift the slender form of his wife into a chair while Gideon assured the curious people who were stopping to stare that there was nothing to see, that everything was all right. By this time Anthea was beginning to stir, opening dazed eyes to look up at her husband.

'I'm sorry, I——'

'What happened, my dear?' Samuel asked worriedly as Anthea had trouble articulating. 'Anthea, talk to me!'

She attempted a smile, straightening in the chair, smiling at the manager of the café as he brought her a refreshing drink. 'I just fainted, Samuel——'

'*Just* fainted?' he repeated incredulously. 'I've never known you to faint before!'

Anthea gave a light laugh, recovering rapidly. 'There has to be a first time for everything. I'm feeling fine now. It was so silly of me.'

'Nevertheless, I think we should get you back and let Michael take a look at you.'

'Yes,' Gideon had managed to dispel the crowd that had gathered, joining them at the table, 'I think so too. You're still looking very pale.'

Merry frowned at how ill Anthea still looked; there was a greyness beneath the tan she had acquired over the last month, her eyes huge and haunted. Anthea might be over her faint, but something was still bothering her deeply.

'Maybe you're right.' Anthea's hand trembled as she pushed back her hair. 'Although I think I'll have to have help getting back, I really do feel really weak.' She looked up at Merry for the first time since she had recovered consciousness, a sheen of tears to her eyes. 'Merry, I—Will you come back with me? Please?' Her voice was husky.

Merry sqallowed hard, seeing the look that passed between father and son, feeling that sense of tension herself. Why had Anthea asked her specifically? Could it be that she suspected something, that that was the reason for the faint?

Merry didn't know whether she felt relief or apprehension that the truth might at last be going to come out.

CHAPTER NINE

'You know, don't you.' Merry's words were a statement, not a question.

The four of them had arrived back at the yacht a few minutes ago, Anthea asking that only Merry accompany her to her cabin, leaving the two men on deck to have a much-needed drink. Neither Gideon nor Samuel had argued with Anthea's request, making Merry wonder if they too realised Anthea might have guessed the truth.

Anthea sat opposite her in the sitting area of her cabin, very pale but composed, her hands clasped together to stop their trembling. 'I—I hope I do,' she said huskily. 'I can't believe it, but I hope it's true.'

Merry swallowed hard, almost as pale as Anthea now. 'You do?' She moistened her lips nervously.

Clear eyes met identical green ones. 'Do you doubt it?'

She chewed on her bottom lip. 'I think for a while I did.'

'Which is why you pretended to be Gideon's girl-friend?'

'Yes.' She didn't attempt to prevaricate, knowing it was too late for that.

Tears flooded Anthea's eyes, her mouth trembled slightly. 'I'm not mad, am I, Merry? You are my daughter.'

Her breathing became shallow. 'I—Yes.' her voice was barely above a whisper.

'Oh, God!' Anthea closed her eyes, a glittering sheen to their depths as she once again looked at Merry. 'I can see it now,' she choked. 'As Gideon's girl-friend it never even occurred to me ... But I'm sure that was the idea,' she sighed. 'Then today, outside the café, you turned and smiled, and I—I suddenly *knew*. I couldn't believe it. It seemed so incredible!'

'Gideon found me,' Merry revealed. 'But I wasn't sure. I——'

'I understand,' Anthea squeezed her hand. 'And I thank Gideon for what he's done.'

'I found it all so incredible too. My father——' Merry stopped, biting her lip.

'Your father?' Anthea prompted huskily.

She couldn't meet her mother's gaze. 'He persuaded me to see you, to meet you.'

Anthea sighed, her expression pained. 'I understand your not wanting to. To all intents and purposes I deserted you when you were a baby.' She saw the embarrassed colour flood Merry's cheeks. 'I can see that you obviously thought so too. And it's the truth,' she admitted heavily.

Merry gave a choked cry, then came down on her knees in front of the other woman, clasping her hands, the tears falling slowly down her cheeks. 'No,' she shook her head. 'My father was right, it was too big a responsibility for a seventeen-year-old girl to cope with.'

'I think,' her mother's voice was shaky, 'that your father must be a very nice man.'

'Oh, he is!'

'And your mother?'

'She was wonderful too. But she's dead now.'

'I'm sorry,' Anthea squeezed her hand again. 'But you've been happy?'

She could hear the deep concern in her mother's voice, knew once again the pain she must have suffered at giving up her baby, needing the reasurance of knowing she had done the right thing. 'I've been very happy,' she told her with a glowing smile. 'Even more so now that I've met you,' she added—and meant it. she liked Anthea, and she believed that in time she would come to love her.

They were suddenly in each other's arms, laughing and crying at the same time. Merry felt as if her heart would burst, and she knew Anthea felt the same way. They were still in each other's arms when Samuel arrived with Michael.

He cleared his throat noisily, obviously affected by the emotional scene he was witnessing.

Michael allowed them all a few minutes to recover before taking over, then he insisted on examining his patient, declaring that Anthea had had enough excitement for one day and that she needed to rest.

Amid much protesting from Anthea Merry promised that she would be back soon to continue their talk, leaving with Michael.

'I have no idea what's going on,' Michael murmured. 'Although I could take a good guess. I haven't seen Anthea this happy in a long time.' he gave her a sideways glance. 'Or you either, for that matter.'

Merry gave a shaky smile. 'I can't tell you anything, Michael. It isn't my secret to tell.'

He gently touched her hand. 'I know a little of Anthea's history, it was necessary for me to. And I think my guess about the two of you would be pretty accurate. I'm pleased for you both.'

'Thank you,' she accepted huskily.

'I'll leave you to be alone now. I'm sure this has shaken you as much as it has Anthea.'

She was grateful for his understanding, desperately needing to be alone to collect her own thoughts together. She didn't doubt that things would be all right between Anthea and herself, although she did still feel a curiosity about her real father, about the circumstances behind her mother being alone and pregnant at seventeen. No doubt she would know it all in time.

She moved to the stern of the yacht, away from the other guests, looking out over Cadiz, allowing the sea breeze to help clear her head. There was no doubting Anthea's joy at finding she was her daughter, and she felt a relief that the pretence was at last over. But it was going to be very strange adjusting to having a mother again.

'Where the hell have you been?' Gideon rasped behind her.

She turned, recoiling at the fury in his face. 'I——'

'I've been looking for you everywhere!' he accused harshly.

Anger burned at the way he was verbally attacking her. No hello, no how are you, just demands. She was in no mood for Gideon's arrogance right now. 'Not here, obviously,' she snapped, her head back in challenge.

'Obviously,' he bit out, his nostrils flared angrily. 'What do you mean by disappearing like that?'

'Don't tell me you've been worried about me?' she taunted.

Anger tightened his face, his eyes glittering dangerously. 'No,' he snapped. 'But I was concerned about Anthea,' he added with cold deliberation. 'My father won't let anyone in their cabin at the moment, and he won't come out either. I want to know what the hell is going on!'

'And you always get what you want, don't you,' Merry said wearily, hating the fact that Gideon could hurt her so easily by just a few cutting words. But this time, as during the last six days, he had hurt her deliberately, taken enjoyment from causing her pain. She had no idea what she could have done to him in return, but he seemed to feel she deserved his anger.

'Not always,' he said curtly. 'What I *want* isn't always good for me.'

Her eyes widened at the edge to his voice, the almost bitter tone. It was almost as if he blamed her for something!

'So,' he bit out. 'Did you tell Anthea who you are?'

She sighed. 'I didn't have to, she'd already guessed.'

'But you confirmed it,' he said grimly.

Merry shrugged and turned away, finding his proximity too overpowering when her defences had already taken such a battering. Why couldn't Gideon have loved her in return, why couldn't he hold her now, tell her that everything was all right, that he would help her through this, that he would always be there to help her?

But he said none of those things, just glared at her as if he heartily disliked her, as if he wished he had never set eyes on her, as if he wished he had run across the same stubborn bureaucrat that his father had, that Harrington had never found her!

'Why deny it?' Her voice was merely a whisper.

'Because we had agreed you wouldn't tell her——'

'You agreed,' she corrected abruptly. 'I don't remember saying anything.'

'Typical woman! Would it have hurt you to have done something *I* wanted you to for a change?'

She had already done far too many things that he wanted her to, some of them she would have been better not doing. In fact, *she* wished Harrington had never found her! She had fallen in love with a man who couldn't possibly love her in the same way, who didn't seem to think he could love any woman with the singlemindedness she craved.

'You don't own me,' she snapped, her eyes blazing.

'Maybe it's time some man did!' Gideon looked just as furious.

'Not you!' she shouted at him.

'Certainly not me,' he scorned. 'Who wants a little hellcat like you around permanently?'

She gave an angry gasp. 'Well, you've got me!' she glared at him furiously. 'I'm *family* now, Gideon. And I'll stay family.'

He pushed roughly past her. 'How fortunate I'm to spend the next year in America, away from my *family*.' With that he walked back to the lounge area, the sound of his husky laugh soon floating in the breeze to taunt her.

PAGAN ENCHANTMENT 155

To say they ignored each other throughout dinner was perhaps putting it a little strongly, but they certainly didn't speak to each other unless they had to.

For Merry it was the most miserable time she had spent since she had first known Gideon. She had realised she meant nothing to him, had thought their meetings would be few once they were off the yacht, but she hadn't realised he intended actually leaving the country for a *year*!

Oh, it was a lifetime! How could she survive without even seeing him, not knowing when he was even in the country again? She had thought that as Anthea's daughter she might be able to at least see him occasionally. She should have known Gideon was much too independent to let family ties keep him from where his work was, in America. His time in England and on the yacht had just been in the nature of a holiday, and when they reached England it would be time to get back to his first and only love, making films.

When her seasickness returned that night she didn't know if her misery was due to that or to the thought that Gideon was soon to disappear from her life for a year.

Whatever it was she felt awful, and the nearer they got to England the worse she felt, the combination of the Atlantic and the Mediterranean meeting in the Bay of Biscay making the sailing very rough.

Anthea spent a lot of time with her during the three days before they reached England, alternately talking to her or helping the weakened Merry to the bathroom when she felt too ill to lie in bed any longer. Of Gideon she saw nothing, and the way she felt she was glad of it. The last thing she needed was for Gideon to see her with her hair all stringy and no colour in her cheeks.

It was during one of their talking sessions together

that Merry dared to ask Anthea about her father, or at least, the man who had fathered her.

Anthea swallowed hard, a dark blush deepening the colour of her cheeks. 'I was stupid, I have no excuse for what happened. I fell in love with a married man.' She couldn't look at Merry. 'When I became pregnant—quite accidentally,' she added hastily, 'I wasn't stupid enough to try and blackmail him like that. Although I did believe I loved him. I thought when I found out I was pregnant that he would leave his wife for me.'

'And he didn't?' Merry prompted.

'No,' Anthea sighed. 'He told me I was a stupid fool and threw me out of his life. I never saw him again.'

'How awful!'

She shook her head. 'I didn't blame him, I still don't. I might only have been seventeen, but I wasn't that naïve. He believed me to be experienced——'

'At seventeen?'

Anthea shrugged. 'It isn't unheard of, not then, and certainly not now. Alan—that was his name,' she blushed, 'he believed I'd taken care there wouldn't be a baby. *I* never even thought about it.'

Merry chewed on her inner lip. 'You never—never thought of keeping me?'

'Of course I thought of it!—I'm sorry,' Anthea was instantly contrite for her vehemence, 'I thought about it all the time, Merry. But I had nothing, no family, no money, no way of surviving with a young baby. It broke my heart to give you up, but I did it. I wanted the best for you, for you to have two parents, a happy childhood, everything you deserved to have.'

'And I had all that. I had it all. But what did you have?' Merry choked.

'At first,' Anthea spoke slowly, 'I had nothing—except the memory of a lovely black-haired baby with the promise of the beauty you now have.' She smiled sadly. 'But eventually I began to put my life together. I did a secretarial course, made sure I acquired good qualificiations, and I didn't let men into my life, ever. Until Samuel,' her expression softened. 'I became his private secretary. But he was determined from the first that I would be much more than that.'

'You love him.' It was a statement.

'Very much,' Anthea replied without hesitation. 'Although when I first started working for him I viewed him with as much suspicion as every other man. But Samual can be very determined, very persuasive. It wasn't long before I knew I loved him, but it took him a little longer to persuade me to marry him.'

'I'd glad you've been very happy with him,' Merry said with a sincerity that couldn't be doubted.

'Do you think I deserved to be?' The other woman sounded bitter.

'Of course!' Merry sounded scandalised.

Anthea sighed. 'I've never thought so. Ever since the day I gave you up I've been haunted by what had happened to you, who you were with, whether or not they loved you as much as I did. And suddenly,' her voice broke, 'my tiny baby is a grown woman, someone who doesn't hate me, who may even give me a chance to show her I care for her even if I have missed the first twenty years of her life.'

'You didn't miss them because you wanted to,' Merry instantly defended her.

'You believe that?'

'I know it,' she said with certainty.

'You'll let me—let me see you when we get back to England?'

'Try and stop me!' she grinned, dispelling Anthea's anxious expression. 'Maybe you would like to meet my father some time, too?' she offered generously. 'I know he'd like that.'

Anthea swallowed hard. 'Are you sure?'

'Very,' she nodded, knowing how her father would feel about this, confident in his love and trust.

'I'd like it too,' Anthea said almost shyly. 'Maybe I could come and see you at work some time as well?'

Merry gave a rueful laugh. 'That might be difficult at the moment. I'm what they call "resting",' she smiled. 'In other words, out of work,' she explained dryly.

'Oh, I know what resting is,' the other woman laughed too. 'Gideon used to do it a lot in the early days.'

Merry grimaced, almost as white as the pillow she lay back against. 'I doubt he would thank you for telling me that.'

'Probably not,' Anthea still smiled. 'And I doubt if directors rest, they probably call it "looking for the right script".'

'Gideon would,' Merry derided.

'You've argued again?' Anthea frowned her concern.

'Doesn't it show?'

'Yes,' Anthea sighed. 'He can be so stubborn, you know, so very stubborn. He's asked how you are every day, but he won't come in and see you himself. But for goodness' sake don't tell him I told you even that!'

'I'm not likely to see him to tell him anything.' Although it pleased her that he had at least asked about her.

'Of course you'll see him,' her mother said briskly. 'You can't go on avoiding each other for ever.'

'Gideon says he's going to America for—for some time.' Merry pleated the sheet beneath her hand.

'Mm,' Anthea nodded. 'But not for a couple of months yet. It's so strange that you should both be in the same profession.'

Merry grimaced. 'I don't think I'm in the same class as Gideon.'

'Of course you are,' the other women defended

indignantly, a selfconscious smile suddenly parting her peach-tinted lips. 'I sound like a doting mother, don't I?' she derided.

Merry giggled. 'A little. But it's nice.'

'You don't mind?'

She hated that vulnerable look in Anthea's eyes, knew how deeply the other woman had come to depend on her love and respect. She hoped and prayed Anthea would never have to feel she had let her down. 'I don't mind at all,' she grinned. 'You'll probably get sick of seeing me once we're back in England. I like to talk to someone when I have a problem, and with my father so far away it isn't always possible to talk to him. How do you feel about listening to my troubles?' she teased lightly.

'I'd love it,' the other woman laughed.

'Good. And talking about feeling sick ...' she swallowed convulsively.

Anthea was instantly on her feet. 'Again?' she said gently.

'I'm afraid so.' Merry staggered to her feet. 'Michael's magic potion doesn't seem to be working this time. How does the yacht sail at this eighty-degree angle?' she groaned.

Anthea laughed softly as she helped her. 'It really isn't that bad.'

Her eyes widened. 'You mean it could get worse?'

'No, I don't think so, not this time,' her mother chuckled.

'I suppose that's something!' Merry stumbled into the bathroom to be sick once again.

But the times she lay in her cabin alone were the worst, when she could occasionally hear Gideon moving about in the next cabin, could hear him but never saw him. He stayed away from her as if she had the plague and not just seasickness, and she knew that it wasn't the latter that kept him away from her, that he had completely washed his hands of her after their last fiery argument.

All the time she was wondering who he was captivating with his charm, which of the women on board he had chosen for his attention. She knew it was no longer Linda, knew from Michael's happiness that his fiancée had at last given up on Gideon to concentrate on him. She was pleased for the doctor, although it didn't stop her worrying who Gideon was flirting with. A couple of the other woman, on more than one occasion, had given the impression that they were more than willing to encourage him. And in his present mood he didn't need much encouragement to behave outrageously.

He seemed to spend little time in his cabin during the day, only usually coming back to change his clothes for dinner, often coming back at the end of the evening in the early hours of the morning.

Consequently Merry was surprised to see him enter her cabin unannnounced on their last day at sea, glad she had got Anthea to help her wash her hair this morning, looking more like her old self as the sea seemed to calm itself the last twenty-four hours or so, although she was still very pale.

'Gideon!' she gasped.

He closed the door forcefully behind him, before walking over to the side of her bed, looking very dark and attractive in a navy blue sweat-shirt and fitted denims, the weather having cooled considerably as they approached England.

He said nothing, but looked down at her with narrowed eyes, and Merry flushed uncomfortably. What had she done now, for goodness' sake? He never seemed to talk to her willingly any more, not unless he had something to berate her about.

Today seemed to be no different!

'I don't appreciate this emotional blackmail,' he snarled suddenly, dangerous lights in the deep blue of his eyes. 'And if you'd known anything about me at all you would know I wouldn't.'

Merry had gasped at the first fierceness of his attack, and sat up straighter against the pillows.

'Using Anthea is not only underhand, it's damned——'

'Using Anthea for what?' she exploded.

'Unprofessional,' he finished as if she hadn't spoken, turning to pace the length of the cabin. 'I've heard of some tricks in my time, but this is definitely the worst. I've had——'

'Will you kindly tell me what you're talking about?' Merry snapped.

'—some things tried on *me* in the past,' once again he continued as if she hadn't spoken. 'I've even had women sleep with me to get into one of my films,' he added disgustedly.

Merry's eyes widened, as his meaning became clearer by the second. 'Are you suggesting——'

'But at least they were honest about what they were doing,' Gideon continued in that angry tone. '*They* didn't go to such lengths to get a job——'

'My God, you are!' she breathed slowly, getting out of the bed now, her cotton nightgown that reached down to the floor being more than adequate covering. 'You're accusing me of using Anthea's influence to get me a part in your film,' she accused angrily.

'Yes!' There was anger in every taut muscle of his body. 'Maybe it wouldn't have been so bad if you *had* been willing to sleep with me——'

'You——'

'But to ask Anthea to speak to me on your behalf,' he finished contemptuously. 'I find that totally unacceptable.'

If Gideon was angry Merry was more so, so much so that she couldn't speak for several seconds. 'You arrogant fool!' she finally burst out, seeing his mouth tighten with fury. 'How dare you come in here and accuse me of—of——'

'Using your relationship with Anthea to get a part in my next film,' he supplied tautly.

Her mouth twisted, and she looked very young in her bare feet, her face free of make-up. 'You're more than an arrogant fool, Gideon,' she bit out. 'You're a *stupid* arrogant fool! I wouldn't appear in one of your films if you were the last director in the world,' she told him with bravado, knowing that to appear in one of his films would make any young unknown actress a star. But not her, not like this!

He gave a derisive, humourless laugh. 'If any of my fellow-directors have heard of your appearance in Anderson's play you may find that's exactly what I am as far as you're concerned!'

'God, I hate you!' she snapped vehemently.

'Believe me,' he ground out harshly, 'the feeling is more than mutual.'

Merry swallowed down her next angry comment, taken aback by the coldness of his tone. 'It would seem,' she hated the betraying quiver in her voice, doing her best to control it when she next spoke, 'it would seem we have nothing more to say to each other.'

'I more than second that.' He flung open the door. 'There will be no part for you in my film!'

'I don't want one!'

'Good!' he slammed out of the cabin.

Merry sank to the floor, crying as if she would never stop. Would loving Gideon always hurt like this? Or would the love, and consequently the pain, eventually fade? God, she hoped so! She couldn't live in this agony for a lifetime.

Still weak from her illness, she cried herself to sleep on the floor, not noticing when she was lifted in gentle arms, knowing nothing of Samuel laying her on the bed, of Anthea smoothing back her hair from her flushed face, of the angry words the latter muttered beneath her breath to the dark man standing beside the door. Gideon turned on his heel and left the room—but he didn't slam it this time.

When Merry eventually woke it was dark outside, only the light over the dressing-table brightening the shadows of the cabin. Anthea sat in the chair beside the bed, smiling gently as Merry opened her eyes to look at her.

'Feeling better?' she prompted.

'I—Oh!' Merry groaned as her body protested achingly at the movement of her legs. 'A bit stiff, I think.'

'Well, if you will fall asleep on the floor . . .' Anthea teased.

Colour darkened her pale cheeks. 'I—er—I did that?' she grimaced.

'Don't you remember?'

'Yes,' she admitted heavily, 'I remember.'

'Gideon was furious, wasn't he,' Anthea stated ruefully.

Her eyes flew open, only to lower her lashes again at the sympathy in Anthea's expression. She couldn't accept pity now, she would break down and cry again if she did.

'If it's any consolation, he was angry with me too,' Anthea told her gently.

Merry looked up at these quietly spoken words. 'He was?'

'Oh yes,' the other woman gave a dry chuckle. 'And he's far from pleasant when he's angry—how silly of me, you know that!' she derided. 'Gideon can be cutting and cruel when he wants to be. And for some reason,' she added thoughtfully, 'he seems to want to be like that with you.'

'He *enjoys* being like that with me,' Merry mumbled, turning away to blink back the tears.

'Yes,' Anthea sighed her agreement. 'And he isn't usually like that with his family——'

'As he's so fond of telling me, I'm not his family!' Merry said vehemently. 'I know you meant well when you—when you talked to Gideon about me, but——'

'But you wish I hadn't. Yes, Gideon made that clear too,' Anthea derided. 'I promise you I won't play the doting mother again,' she was suddenly serious. 'And really, I didn't do so much this time, just mentioned to Gideon that you were out of work, and that he had this new film coming up. Not that I wanted to lose you to America, but Gideon does direct rather good films. I wanted that for you, that's all,' she finished lamely.

'I know that,' Merry nodded. 'But Gideon dislikes me, and working with me is the last thing he wants. He made sure I knew that.'

'He's a fool,' Anthea shook her head.

Merry gave a wan smile. 'I've already told him that.'

Anthea smiled. 'Good for you! Well, don't worry, you won't have to put up with his boorish behaviour again. We dock tomorrow, and Samuel and I will drive you back to London. Gideon is making other arrangements.'

'I—Thank you,' Merry accepted jerkily, wondering what the 'other arrangements' were.

She soon had her answer. Gideon was driving back to London with Michael and Linda.

She didn't see him to talk privately to, just made her general parting from him like everyone else did. He made no effort to say more than goodbye to her, and as she left with Anthea and Samuel she knew that was exactly what it was—goodbye.

CHAPTER TEN

LONDON didn't seem to have changed, still the same hustle and bustle, the same round of parties, the same good friends. Only Merry had changed—beyond all recognition, it seemed to her at times. Her life carried on exactly as it had before she went on the cruise, and yet none of it was the same; *she* wasn't the same.

Her weekly visits to Anthea became the highlight of her life; all the time she was hoping—and equally dreading—that Gideon might be at the town house in the suburbs of London, that she might meet him in that casual way.

And she never did. Six weeks, six whole weeks, and she hadn't seen him, not in the flesh anyway. Magazines and newspapers seemed to be full of the fact that he was auditioning for his next film, speculating even more over his relationship with the beautiful actress Trina Gomez, the black-eyed, black-haired Mexican beauty who was very much in evidence at Gideon's side during the evenings, the fact that she had a husband not seeming to bother either of them.

But it bothered Merry. It didn't seem like the Gideon she had fallen in love with. Yes, he could be cruel and autocratic, but he had made his opinion of attached ladies very clear on more than one occasion.

She burned with jealousy over Trina Gomez's part in his life, although both she and Anthea steered clear of the subject of Gideon during her visits. And if Samuel should happen to be at home too, his business interests usually keeping him very busy, she tried to hide the pain his similarity to Gideon caused her.

Her father and Anthea had met, a tearful occasion on Merry's part, and she was amazed at how easily these two so-different people fell into an easy friendship, her father's liking and respect for Anthea being so obviously reciprocated.

And so she should have been the happiest person alive, the question of her parenthood somehow settled, having a father and a mother, and yet in a strangely different way from others. But it worked, and Samuel treated her like a daughter too, although so far no open declaration had been made as to her being Anthea's daughter—at her insistence. She wasn't sure she was ready yet to fully enter the world of affluence and sophistication as anyone's illegitimate child. She had only just become used to the idea herself. But it was finally the thought of seeing Gideon again that made her agree to the party Anthea and Samuel wanted to give to introduce her formally to all their friends. Surely Gideon couldn't refuse to come to such a party?

He didn't, assuring Anthea by telephone that he would be there. Merry lived in a state of anticipation all week as she waited for Saturday evening and seeing Gideon again to come round. Even if he virtually ignored her, as he had on the day they had parted, she would at least be able to look at him.

At least she was working, so that took her mind off the party a little, having managed to get a small part in a new television series being filmed at Surrey at the moment, the girl originally chosen to play the part having to drop out because of pregnancy.

She enjoyed the experience enormously, knew by the reaction of the more experienced actors that she was playing the part well. It seemed it was only around Gideon she couldn't act.

Late Friday evening, as they finished for the day, Bob Hassall, the director, came into the dressing-room with another man, younger, very confident of his fair good looks.

'Mr Brookes would like to talk to you, Merry,' the director told her, obviously not too pleased with having to perform such a lowly task as introducing this man to the most inexperienced member of his acting team. He left them with an abrupt nod of his head.

Merry frowned at the young man. She had seen him about the studio for about a week now, although no effort had been made to introduce him to the cast. She put her hands selfconsciously in the back pockets of her denims, already changed to go to the station and get her train back to London, her tee-shirt unconsciously stretching across the taut pertness of her breasts.

Simon Brookes smiled at her, instantly looking younger than the late twenties, early thirties she judged him to be. He was dressed as casually as she, if anything his denims were even tighter than hers, leaving nothing to the imagination; his shirt was body-hugging too, his trainers of a similar make and style to her own.

'Can I give you a life back to London?' he offered.

'I——'

'Bob Hassall would hardly have left me alone with you if he didn't think I could be trusted,' he taunted as she was obviously about to refuse.

She smiled. 'Bob is a nice man, but he hardly notices the world about him.' The middle-aged director was single-minded in his dedication to his work. She shrugged. 'I have no idea who you are.'

'My name means nothing to you!' he said with feigned tragedy. 'I, my dear Meredith, am the man who is going to whisk you away from all this to America and stardom.'

'Oh no, you're not,' she laughed, liking this man in spite of herself.

'Just think of it—Hollywood, your name in lights, recognised wherever you go.'

She giggled at the mockery in his voice. 'Don't you mean struggling in some bed-sit in the rough part of town, so desperate for a job that you do virtually anything to get it?'

'Anything?' he smiled hopefully.

'Look, Mr Brookes——'

'Simon——'

'Simon,' she conceded. '*Who* are you? And don't tell me the man who's going to make me a star, I've heard it all before.'

'You have?' his brows rose. 'Tell me more.'

'Certainly not,' she laughed. 'Just tell me *who* you are!'

'I'm on the look-out for someone to play in a film that I'm involved in that goes into production in a couple of months' time.' He was suddenly serious.

Merry's eyes widened. 'And you've chosen me?'

'Not exactly,' he corrected gently. 'I've been watching you the last week, and I'd like you to come to the studio and audition for the part.'

'Why me?' She shook her head in puzzlement.

Simon smiled. 'Most people ask when,' he derided.

'And so do I,' she said hastily. 'Don't misunderstand me, I'd love to audition.' Work on the series finished in six weeks as far as she was concerned, and she would be out of work again then. A part in a film would be a dream come true. And she would be in America, where Gideon was going to be too . . . 'I just don't understand why me,' she frowned. 'My agent never mentioned you, and I've never seen you before, so how did you get my name?'

'Let's just say an interested party told me about you.'

'Interested party?'

'You're a suspicious little thing, aren't you? he smiled. 'Don't question the how of it, Meredith, just accept it.'

'But——'

'Let me drive you home,' he interrupted briskly. 'Then we can talk about it on the way to London. I'm perfectly safe, Meredith,' he encouraged as she still hesitated. 'I could show you my Equity card.'

'Some recommendation!' she chuckled, as she collected her handbag, deciding she was acting like some Victorian maiden. 'Okay, I'll trust you. But I should warn you I went to Judo classes as a child,' she eyed him mockingly.

'Black belt?' Simon enquired as they left the studio together.

'Brown.'

He smiled. 'Black.' He looked proud of himself.

'I'll trust you anyway,' she laughed.

He unlocked the passenger side of the dark green Jaguar and went round to get in beside her.

It took Merry some minutes to unwind after the rigours of the day, and although she was deeply interested in what Simon had to tell her, she rested her head back wearily for several minutes.

'Better?' Simon prompted gently when she at last opened her eyes.

'Better,' she nodded, sitting up. 'Tell me about the audition.'

He nodded. 'You would play the part of a girl caught in the middle of her parent's divorce——'

'Aren't I a little old for that?'

'I was told you look sixteen, and you do.'

'Thanks!'

'It was a compliment. I can think of plenty of women

who would give anything to have your youth. Anyway, the part isn't big, just a secondary one, in fact. But I think it could be quite a good stepping-stone for you.'

'I'm sure of it,' she nodded, feeling the adrenalin starting to flow once again. 'Are you auditioning many other girls?'

'A few,' he confirmed. 'But I think you have a good chance.'

'When would I have to come?' She chewed on her lower lip, knowing that she was committed to the television series for now.

He gave her a sideways glance. 'I already checked with Bob, and he doesn't need you on Monday afternoon.'

Her eyes widened. 'Do you usually organise people in this arrogant way?'

'Always.' He stopped the car outside her home at her directions. 'It saves time.' He gave her the name of the studio. 'Be there about three. Just ask for me.'

Merry took the card he held out to her, putting it in her bag. 'I'll see you on Monday, then.'

'Yes. And don't be late. Our director dislikes unpunctuality.'

'I'll remember.' She waved to him as he accelerated the car away.

She was still looking dazed when she entered the flat, never having had a part come to her before, always having to fight and claw her way just into the interview.

'Good day, love?' Vanda came out of the kitchen, waving a fork about in her hand. 'Shepherd's pie all right?'

'Fine,' Merry, replied absently.

Vanda made a dash for the kitchen as a loud hissing noise and burning smell permeated the lounge.

'Damned potatoes,' she mumbled as she came back, having discarded the fork somewhere along the way. She flung herself down in a chair, one leg dangling over the side. '*Did* you have a good day?'

'Yes—I think.' She gave a rueful smile. 'Yes, I think I did.' She told her friend about Simon Brookes. 'Do you know him?' she frowned.

Her friend shrugged. 'Never heard of him.'

'I've never had anything like this happen to me before,' Merry laughed softly. 'Even if I don't get the part it was a novel experience. How's the play going?' The last few weeks she and Vanda had only met in passing, usually at dinner, as Merry was out working all day and Vanda was at the theatre until late evening, having landed a part in a play in the West End, a walk-on part she called it, but at least it was work.

'It will probably go on for years,' Vanda grimaced. 'But I won't. I've asked Sidney,' she named their agent, 'to try and find me something a little more interesting. I can't keep saying "Yes, ma'am, no, ma'am" for the next five years!'

Merry laughed, then got up to help her friend with the dinner. 'Will you have time from this hectic schedule to come shopping with me in the morning? I have to get a new dress for tomorrow night.'

'I'd love it,' her friend beamed. 'It was nice of your mother to invite me to join you later.'

'You're my friend. Besides, I need some moral support.'

The dress she wore gave her some of that support, being virginal white, fitting smoothly over her breasts, gathered in at the waist with a gold belt and falling in delicate folds to her ankles. Her hair had been professionally secured on top of her head, smooth and gleaming, and she had had a manicure while she had been at the beauty salon, applying her own light make-up.

'You look lovely, Merry.' Vanda kissed her hurriedly on the cheek. 'Good luck! I'll see you later.'

As she took a taxi to the Steeles' house Merry wished she had someone to keep her company, to be at her side when she walked in to the curious stares of all Anthea's friends, her father having declined the invitation saying it was Anthea's night.

Anthea and Samuel were waiting at the door to greet her, alleviating some of her nervousness, and it seemed as if the announcement of her being Anthea's daughter had already been made, and everyone was surprisingly welcoming.

Except Gideon. He hadn't arrived yet, and she could tell by the anxious glances Anthea kept directing at the door that she was afraid he wouldn't come at all.

By ten o'clock Merry had given up the idea herself, and a lot of her enjoyment in the evening faded as she realised she had worked herself up into a state of tension for nothing. Damn the man! Damn, damn, *damn* him!

She was talking to Samuel when she felt a prickling sensation at the back of her neck, a strange shiver down her spine, and her breath caught in her throat as she saw Samuel's face tauten into grim lines.

'I'll kill him,' he muttered fiercely. 'How dare he bring that—that woman to one of Anthea's parties!'

Merry turned slowly, almost afraid of what she might see. Gideon had just come into the room, looking as handsome and distinguished as ever, the exquisitely beautiful Trina Gomez clinging to his arm, her fiery eyes flashing up at him in mute invitation, her straight jet black hair reaching almost down to her waist, the red glittering dress she wore clinging lovingly to each voluptuous curve of her body.

Merry felt Samuel brush past her as he went over to greet the couple, feeling the anger emanating from him. Her own feelings were ones of despair, and she turned away, her hands clasped together to stop them trembling. Samuel was right, how dared Gideon bring that woman to this party, to the party given for *her*! How could he? How could he!

'Merry!'

Only one person said her name in quite that way, Gideon's husky tones were as well known to her as her own. She took a deep steadying breath before turning, steeling herself to face the woman who clung so possessively to his arm.

Gideon was alone, his expression shuttered as he looked down at her. He seemed tired to Merry, his tan having faded somewhat, and there were lines of weariness about his eyes and mouth.

'How are you, little sister?' he taunted.

That broke the spell of seeing him again, her eyes flashing deeply green. This particular joke had worn a little thin on the yacht, it was totally unacceptable now. 'I'm just fine, *big brother*,' she mocked. 'How are you?' She could see Trina Gomez now, could see how she was charming the anger right out of Samuel as she flirted up at him, somehow managing to charm Anthea too.

'Almost ready to leave for the States,' he grated. 'I've brought you a present.'

'Indeed?' Merry remained haughty.

'Yes,' he mocked, handing her a familiar flat jewellery case. 'And please don't give them back this time,' he added softly. 'It's only fitting that I should welcome my new sister into the family.'

'Will you stop——' She broke off, biting her lip.

'Stop what?' Gideon took the gold and diamond necklace out of the velvet-lined box, setting the latter aside to turn her gently away from him. The necklace felt cold against her skin as he draped it about her throat, his fingers impersonal as he fixed the clasp. 'Stop calling you sister?' he murmured softly, his hands resting lightly on her bare shoulders. 'Why should I? That's exactly what you are now. Here,' he turned her slowly, clipping the earrings on to her lobes. 'You look lovely,' he told her huskily.

She moistened her lips nervously, seeing his gaze riveted to the movement, colour flooding her cheeks as she remembered his reaction once before when she had done that. Her mouth instantly tightened.

Gideon straightened, the mockery back in his eyes. 'How's the career going, Merry?'

She stiffened, knowing his opinion of her talents. 'Very well, thank you.'

'Are you working at the moment?'

'Yes,' she snapped. 'And I'm going to America to appear in a film soon,' she exaggerated defensively.

His brows rose. 'Really?'

'Oh yes,' she said airily.

'Anthea hasn't mentioned it.'

'No, well, I—I only found out myself today,' she improvised.

He nodded. 'Is it a good part?'

'Very good,' she nodded. 'Maybe I'll see you while I'm over there?'

'Maybe,' he drawled. 'Although America is a big place.'

'Yes,' she acknowledged heavily, all hopes of the possibility of seeing him in America if she did get the part fading. She knew the fact that Gideon would be in the States at the same time had been more than half the attraction of the part in the film to her. 'Still, it's a possibility,' she added hopefully.

'A possibility,' he conceded, watching the gentle sway of Trina Gomez's body as she walked towards them.

'Gideon,' the Mexican woman said his name with a strangely attractive inflection. 'I like your parents very much,' she smiled.

Merry felt dazzled by the other woman's beauty. Her teeth were very white against her dark complexion. The warmth in her brown flashing eyes spoke of a passionate nature, that desire that was now concentrated on Gideon. Merry's misery deepened as she realised she was no competition for the other woman.

'And this is your little sister,' Trina now looked at her, only genuine interest in the beautiful face.

'Yes, this is Merry,' he supplied abruptly.

Merry thought she should explain the situation, knowing the hunger in her eyes every time she dared look at Gideon needed some explaining. Trina Gomez was too physical a woman herself not to know how Merry felt about Gideon. 'Gideon is only my stepbrother,' she said huskily. 'My mother is married to his father.'

'Ah,' Trina nodded her satisfaction with this, 'now I understand.'

Merry wished she did. The other woman actually seemed relieved that she and Gideon weren't actually related by blood. If Merry were in the same position she wouldn't have been pleased at all!

She was so deeply in thought that she had missed what Gideon was saying, realising he was talking to her. 'I'm sorry?' she blinked up at him.

His mouth tightened. 'I said enjoy the rest of the evening, Merry.'

'I—You're going?'

'Yes,' he nodded. 'I didn't really have the time for this at all. But if I hadn't come the gossips would have surmised that I resent my new sister,' he derided.

And didn't he? Wasn't resentment a large part of his dislike of her? Oh, not for any feelings of parental jealousy, Gideon just didn't like her; he had only come here tonight for Anthea's sake.

She tentatively wetted her suddenly dry lips, too miserable to notice the darkening of deep blue eyes. 'I— Will I see you again before you go to America?'

'You may do,' Gideon answered uninterestedly. 'Ready, Trina?' He turned to the Mexican woman.

'Yes, I am ready,' she smiled warmly at Merry. 'I am very pleased to have met you.'

Merry could feel no dislike towards the other woman; she found she actually liked her. If only she weren't Gideon's latest mistress!

She watched as the other couple left, Gideon's head bent low as he talked softly to the Mexican woman, his arm about her waist. Merry turned away to hide her pain.

'It's all fiction, you know.'

She looked up to find Michael at her side. 'What is?' she choked, finding Michael's undoubted contentment in his month-long marriage to Linda a painful reminder of what she would never have.

'Gideon and Trina,' he derided.

'It looked far from fiction to me!'

'Ah, but you were only seeing what you were meant to see,' he smiled at her puzzled frown. 'Would it help any if I told you Trina is a married lady——'

'I already know that!'

'A *happily* married lady,' he added pointedly. 'With four little Gomezes.'

She swallowed hard. 'Four?' The other woman didn't look old enough to have four children.

He nodded. 'At the last count. Of course that was a year or so ago, there may be another one by now.'

'I—I don't understand,' Merry frowned.

'I don't think you were supposed to,' Michael said thoughtfully. 'Poor Gideon, he must be in the last throes,' he added enigmatically, laughing as he saw the utter confusion on her face. 'You don't have the faintest idea what I'm talking about, do you?'

'No,' she admitted frankly.

He shook his head. 'And I don't think I should be the one to tell you. I just want you to know that Trina is a very happily married woman, to her childhood sweetheart, that she has been since she was sixteen. Her husband just happens to be a man who likes to stay out of the limelight. Besides, someone has to take care of all those children,' he teased.

'So you don't think she and Gideon——' She couldn't finish the question.

'I know they aren't,' Michael dismissed with certainty. 'She's just—camouflage.'

'You aren't making much sense, you know,' Merry said impatiently.

'One day it will all be clear to you, my dear,' he teased in a mysterious voice. 'I can hardly wait!' he added with relish. 'Poor Gideon doesn't know when he's beaten,' he chuckled.

'Gideon's never beaten!'

'He has been this time,' Michael grinned. 'He's just not ready to admit it yet.' And with that enigmatic statement he led her over to where Linda was chatting to another couple, looking obviously as ecstatic about being his wife as he was at being her husband. Whatever Linda had felt for Gideon she was certainly over it now, having eyes only for Michael. Merry had even found herself liking Linda tonight.

But the whole evening had fallen flat for her after Gideon's departure, although she put a brave face on it for Anthea's sake, knowing the party had been a success in what it had set out to do, and that was to introduce her to all her mother's friends.

But when—or would she ever, see Gideon again?

In the end it was a bit of a rush for Merry to get to the audition on time, as the schedule for the filming of the series changed suddenly on Monday morning, requiring that she shoot two important scenes before she could leave.

She arrived at the studio in London fifteen minutes late for her audition, feeling hot, sticky and untidy, knowing she looked it too. She was so late they probably wouldn't even let her do it now!

The girl at the reception desk didn't seem to feel that was the case, and rang through to one of the offices in the depths of the building to announce Merry's arrival.

'If you'll just take a seat, Miss Charles,' she smiled up at Merry several seconds later, 'someone will be down for you in just a moment.'

Merry took advantage of the time to brush her hair and put on some lip-gloss, forcing herself to calm down. After all, she was still going to get the audition by the look of it.

To her surprise it was Simon Brookes himself who came down for her, smiling his greeting, obviously pleased to see her. Merry launched into a rapid tale about why she was late.

'Calm down,' Simon chided teasingly. 'When it looked as if you weren't going to turn up I rang Bob Hassall, and he explained about the change in schedule.' He led her over to the lift.

'And you waited for me?' Her eyes were wide.

'Of course,' he nodded.

'The part hasn't gone yet?'

'Not yet.' He preceded her out of the lift and into a darkened studio, with only the stage lit up.

Merry viewed it nervously, for some reason feeling it was very important that she do well at this audition.

A young male actor stood up as she followed Simon on to the stage, shooting her a curious glance. Merry nodded to him nervously, receiving a friendly smile in return.

'Let's get on with it,' a voice rasped from the darkness of the seating area. 'I haven't got all day to waste!'

Merry stiffened at the sound of the voice, although it sounded strangely hollow in the largeness of the studio. She shook her head, turning her attention to what Simon was telling her about the scene she was to play. She would hear bells in her head soon, and see fairies at the bottom of the garden—if she had one, that was.

Simon was explaining the build-up to the scene, the row with her parents, the feelings of rejection, her turning to a man for the affection she craved. He introduced the man who was to play the scene with her as Patrick O'Shea.

'Welsh, are you?' Merry joked.

'Scottish,' Patrick grinned.

The two of them laughed together over his obviously Irish name.

'Good luck,' Simon told her softly.

'We're waiting,' that hollow-sounding voice echoed from the back of the studio as Simon went to sit in the front row.

Merry frowned once again. Surely it couldn't be——

'Merry!' Simon prompted impatiently.

'I—er—Sorry.' She picked up the script and checked through it. 'Ready,' she nodded to Patrick.

To say she played the part of her life would be an overstatement, but she was good, she knew she was. She had to be in with a chance, at least, she thought triumphantly as they came to the end of the scene.

She turned with an excited smile to Simon, her words freezing in her throat as she saw the man walking down the central aisle. She hadn't been cracking up at all, that autocratic voice barking orders from the back of the studio *did* belong to Gideon!

She could read none of his thoughts from his expression as he bent to speak softly to Simon, and she wasn't spared a second glance as he straightened to walk out of the studio.

She couldn't believe it. She had just auditioned for Gideon's film, and after telling him she already had the part. How he must have been laughing at her! Well, she didn't need to be told she hadn't got the part, she knew exactly what Simon was going to say to her when he reached her side, knew that Gideon would think Anthea had arranged this. And perhaps she had, perhaps she was the 'interested party' Simon had mentioned last week.

'You were very good, Merry——'

She didn't wait for the 'but' part of the conversation, turning blazing green eyes on Simon.' 'Where has Gideon gone?' she demanded to know.

He frowned. 'To his office——'

'Where is it?' she snapped.

'Up a floor and the third door on the left. But——'

'Excuse me,' she said abruptly. 'I have to talk to him.' She didn't wait to hear any more of Simon's objections, but rushed from the room, getting in the lift and going up to Gideon's office, not bothering to knock before throwing open the cream-coloured door, not caring who Gideon was with. He was going to listen to her!

He sat behind a huge leather-topped desk, the whole of London stretched out behind him through the window, papers and scripts scattered all over the room, reminding Merry of how untidy he was. He was alone.

She didn't wait for him to speak, but marched over to stand facing him across the desk. 'I was good!' she told him vehemently. 'You have no right to refuse me just because of who I am. And if Anthea did arrange all this, I can tell you——'

'She didn't,' he stated calmly.

That took the wind out of her sails. 'You know that?' she gulped.

'Yes. Because I arranged it myself.' He met her gaze challengingly, the dark blue shirt stretched tautly across his shoulders, his denims tight-fitting.

She blinked dazedly. 'You did?'

'Yes.'

'But I—Why, Gideon? Did you want so badly to humiliate me?' Tears filled her eyes. 'Do you hate me so much that you put me through that just to give the part to someone else?' she choked.

'I don't hate you at all,' he told her calmly. 'And there are no other girls to give the part to. You're the only one who was auditioned.'

'But Simon said—I don't understand,' she shook her head.

'Neither do I,' he frowned. 'Didn't Simon tell you you have the part?'

'No, he—I didn't give him much time to say anything. I—I wanted to talk to you.'

'What about?' he asked coldly.

The things he was saying were completely unnerving her, she couldn't even think straight. 'I thought—I didn't think—*Why* did you arrange it, Gideon?' she asked breathlessly. 'I thought you said I couldn't act?'

'I've never said that,' he denied abruptly. 'Bob Hassall let me see the previews of *House of Grant*,' he named the television series they were just filming. 'You're very good. And the performance you gave just now was excellent.'

'So I—I have the part?' she gulped.

'You have the part,' he nodded. 'Although I have to say that you would have got the part whether or not you were good.'

'I would?'

'Yes. You'll join us on location in two months' time.'

'Oh.' Merry didn't know what else to say, her head was spinning. 'I thought perhaps Anthea had arranged it all. I really had no idea you were going to be here today.'

His mouth twisted. 'That was obvious from what you said on Saturday. I was surprised to hear you already had the part,' he mocked.

'Yes, well . . .' she blushed. 'That was self-defence.'

He sat forward, suddenly tense. 'Why?'

She shrugged. 'You've always seemed so derisive of my acting ability. I felt I had to defend myself.'

Gideon sighed. 'How did you put up with me, Merry?' He rested his elbows on the desk, his fingers massaging his temples as if they ached. 'I've been a bastard to you.' He shook his head.

Her eyes widened. 'No——'

'Oh yes,' he insisted grimly. 'And I'm not proud of it.'

'You don't have to give me a part in your film out of remorse!' she told him heatedly.

He looked at her with darkened blue eyes. 'I'm giving you the part because you can do it. I knew you could do it. I also want you close to me,' he added softly.

Merry sat down suddenly in the chair facing him. 'W-why?'

'Because I love you. And I want you to love me in return,' he stated simply.

'But I—What about Trina Gomez?' she gasped, not able to believe what she was hearing.

Gideon stood up to come round the desk, leaning back against it, only inches away from her now, his aura of masculinity reaching out to capture her. 'She's the star of the new film, and a little exposure never does any harm. Besides, she knew how I felt about you, and she didn't mind helping me out with a little——'

'Camouflage,' Merry said, suddenly knowing what Michael had meant Saturday night.

Gideon frowned. 'Camouflage?'

'It's something Michael said,' she dismissed absently.

'Indeed?' Gideon drawled, his voice hardening.

'Yes. He—he also said something about you being in the last throes,' she looked at him intently. 'And that you don't know when you're beaten.'

'Did he indeed?' Gideon mused derisively. 'Well, he's wrong. I *do* know when I'm beaten. And I went through the last throes weeks ago. I admit defeat, I admit I love you wildly. I also admit that now I have you coming to work with me I'm going to do my best to make you love me in return.'

'But all those other women you've—you've——'

'Slept with. Had sex with,' he finished abruptly. 'They're still there if I want them. But I don't. And I'm not interested in unemotional sex any more either. You're still a child in a lot of ways, Merry, and may not understand all of what I'm telling you, but having sex with a woman is no longer enough for me, I want to make love—with you, only with you. I want to make love *to* you, desperately in fact, but I also want to just be with you, talk with you, be silent with you, grow old with you.' His mouth twisted. 'Although I'll do that a little quicker than you will, especially with a young wife to keep in line! But I want all that, Merry,' he was suddenly serious again, 'and I'm not going to rest until

I have it. You'll never escape me. I want children with you too, black-haired, green-eyed little witches like their mother.'

She might still be partly a child, as he said she was, but she was adult enough to understand each beautiful word he was telling her, to know that for her Gideon would make the ultimate commitment, that he had already made that commitment, that he couldn't stop loving her now if he wanted to. And he didn't want to!

She stood up to move in between his parted legs, resting her body against his. 'Or black-haired, blue-eyed devils like their father,' she said huskily, her arms going up about his neck.

His throat moved convulsively. 'Merry——'

'I love you too, Gideon,' she smiled lovingly. 'I love you so much. From the beginning, it seems.'

He was searching her face with disbelieving eyes, almost afraid to believe what she was saying, although his arms came about her possessively. 'You're sure?'

She gave an exultant laugh. 'Very.'

'Oh God, darling...!' His mouth claimed hers, not roughly as she had expected, but with a gentle reverence that told her better than words how much he loved her. He rested his forehead on hers. 'I've been so bloody-minded, so damned cruel to you at times. And I've been so jealous of every man that comes near you—even my father.'

'Samuel?' she echoed in amazement.

'Yes,' he admitted ruefully. 'If he danced with you or spoke to you. And as for Michael...! And you shouldn't accept lifts from strangers,' he added grimly. 'Simon could have been anyone. I could have wrung your neck when he told me he had driven you back to London. And Patrick O'Shea is lucky to still be standing,' he growled.

'You were jealous of *him*?' She was incredulous.

Gideon nodded. 'You were laughing with him, something you never seemed to do with me. I didn't like it. And I didn't like him kissing you during that scene either,' he scowled. 'I'm going to be hell to work with during this film,' he added ruefully.

'Then I won't take the part.' She caressed his rigid jaw.

'You damn well will,' he told her adamantly. 'I told you, you're good.'

'But if it's going to worry you——'

'You'll be my wife long before that, Merry,' he said huskily. 'I'll know it's me you're coming home with at night. I've discovered this blind jealousy within myself the last two months, on the yacht and since, always wondering who you were with, what you were doing, if you were missing me half as much as I missed you...'

'You could have come and seen me.' She lovingly brushed back a lock of dark hair from his forehead.

'No,' he grimaced.

'Those last throes?' she teased gently.

'I'm afraid so. Do you know when I first realised I loved you?' his hands caressed the base of her spine as he held her to him.

'Tell me.' She began to kiss his throat.

'It was—God!' he groaned, his body hardening with desire as her tongue searched the hollows of his throat. 'It was the night you and my father decided Anthea should be told the truth.' His voice wasn't quite steady as desire surged through his body. 'I suddenly realised that if you did I would have no further excuse to touch you, to kiss you, to be with you. I didn't want that to come to an end, and I was vicious with you about it. But I suddenly didn't want the kisses to stop. When they did I had to stay away from you completely or risk making love to you against your will.'

'Did I act as if I would fight you?' she mocked.

He shrugged. 'Physical desire is completely different from falling in love with someone. And when the two happen together...! God, it's agony,' he groaned. 'Then Anthea suggested I might have a part for you in this film.'

'And you lost your temper with me,' she murmured just below his ear, slowly unbuttoning his shirt.

'Only because the idea had been going through my mind already! I loved you, but I wasn't willing to admit it then, and I resented anyone trying to manipulate me. God, Merry...' he groaned as she caressed his chest with her mouth. 'Who taught you to kiss like this?' he moaned.

'You did,' she chuckled.

'So I did,' he said achingly. 'I love you, darling. I promise to love you all my life. Will you marry me?'

'Oh yes!' She met his gaze, her eyes glowing with an inner fire. 'But there will be no more Trina Gomezes in your life, not even for publicity.'

'Only a Merry Steele, hmm?' he teased. 'I like the sound of that,' he said huskily. 'I like the sound of that a lot.'

And when Simon Brookes came in search of them a few minutes later he could see Merry liked it too, that she more than liked it. He very wisely left, unnoticed by either of them, their absorption in each other complete.

The romantic gift for Christmas

First time in paperback, four superb romances by favourite authors, in an attractive special gift pack. A superb present to give. And to receive.

United Kingdom £3.80
Publication 14th October 1983

Darkness of the Heart
Charlotte Lamb

Virtuous Lady
Madeleine Ker

ust in Summer Madness
Carole Mortimer

Man-Hater
Penny Jordan

ook for this gift pack where you buy Mills & Boon romances

Mills & Boon.
The rose of romance.

An orchestra for you

In the Rose of Romance Orchestra, conducted by Jack Dorsey of '101 Strings' fame, top musicians have been brought together especially to reproduce in music the moods and sounds of Romance.

The Rose of Romance Orchestra brings you classic romantic songs like Yours, Just the Way You Are, September Song and many others.

We promise you a new dimension of pleasure and enjoyment as you read your favourite romances from Mills & Boon.

Volumes 1 & 2 now available on the Rose Records label wherever good records are bought.

Usual price £3.99 (Record or Cassette)

Mills & Boon

The rose of romance.

A wonderful **new** service from **Mills & Boon**

Your very own Horoscope

ONLY £5

Discover the real you

Mills & Boon are offering you this special chance to discover what it is that makes you tick — your emotions — your strengths — your weaknesses and how you appear to others.

A 6,000 word horoscope will be prepared for you using the latest computer techniques. The interpretation is written under the guidance of the UK's leading astrologers.

For just £5.00 you will receive

- A full birth chart
- A list of planetary aspects
- A detailed 6,000 word character analysis
- A monthly forecast of your year ahead **or** — for an extra £3.50 — a forecast of the principle trends for the next ten years.

... all beautifully bound and presented in an attractive lilac folder.

The perfect gift!

Simply fill in the coupon below and send it with your cheque or postal order made payable to 'Horoscope Offer', P.O. Box 20, Tunbridge Wells, Kent TN4 9NP.

Please allow 28 days for delivery.

TO: MILLS & BOON HOROSCOPE SERVICE   10HS
PLEASE USE BLOCK CAPITALS

NAME: MR/MRS/MISS ....

ADDRESS ....

....

....

My birth information is:

Place .... County ....

Country .... Date .... Time .... am/pm
(If time unknown we will use midday)

Please send me .... qty)

1 year horoscope at £5.00
10 year horoscope at £8.50
I enclose cheque/P.O. for £ ....

Overseas
Add £1.00 extra for postage and packing

ROMANCE

Next month's romances from Mills & Boon

Each month, you can choose from a world of variety in romance with Mills & Boon. These are the new titles to look out for next month.

CHAINS OF REGRET Margaret Pargeter
BELOVED STRANGER Elizabeth Oldfield
SUBTLE REVENGE Carole Mortimer
MARRIAGE UNDER FIRE Daphne Clair
A BAD ENEMY Sara Craven
SAVAGE ATONEMENT Penny Jordan
A SECRET INTIMACY Charlotte Lamb
GENTLE PERSUASION Claudia Jameson
THE FACE OF THE STRANGER Angela Carson
THE TYZAK INHERITANCE Nicola West
TETHERED LIBERTY Jessica Steele
NO OTHER CHANCE Avery Thorne

Buy them from your usual paperback stockist, or write to: Mills & Boon Reader Service, P.O. Box 236, Thornton Rd, Croydon, Surrey CR9 3RU, England. Readers in South Africa-write to: Mills & Boon Reader Service of Southern Africa, Private Bag X3010, Randburg, 2125.

Mills & Boon
the rose of romance

ROMANCE

Variety is the spice of romance

Each month, Mills & Boon publish new romances. New stories about people falling in love. A world of variety in romance – from the best writers in the romantic world. Choose from these titles in October.

PAGAN ENCHANTMENT Carole Mortimer
FOR PRACTICAL REASONS Claudia Jameson
AN ATTRACTION OF OPPOSITES Sandra Field
TROPICAL TEMPEST Flora Kidd
THE GIRL AT COBALT CREEK Margaret Way
NEVER SAY GOODBYE Betty Neels
SEASON OF FORGETFULNESS Essie Summers
HAUNTED Charlotte Lamb
GILDED CAGE Catherine George
A FIERCE ENCOUNTER Jane Donnelly
TURBULENT COVENANT Jessica Steele
VOYAGE OF THE MISTRAL Madeleine Ker

On sale where you buy paperbacks. If you require further information or have any difficulty obtaining them, write to: Mills & Boon Reader Service, PO Box 236, Thornton Road, Croydon, Surrey CR9 3RU, England.

Mills & Boon
the rose of romance

SIX MAGNIFICENT SOLITAIRE DIAMOND RINGS FROM JAMES WALKER MUST BE WON EACH WORTH £1,000

IN THE MILLS & BOON
Romantic Partner COMPETITION

Simply study the nine famous names from literary romances listed A to I below and match them (by placing letter in the appropriate box) to their respective partners. Then in not more than 12 words complete the tie breaker in an apt and original manner, fill in your name and address, together with the store where you purchased this book and send it to:

Larger actual

**Mills & Boon Romantic Partners Competition
6 Sampson Street, London E1 9NA.**

The six winners will each receive a magnificent solitaire diamond ring, worth* £1,000 (retail value) specially selected from the wide range available at James Walker the jewellers.
*Correct at time of going to print as valued by James Walker, Jewellers.

RULES

1. The competition is open to residents of the UK and Eire only, aged 16 years and over, other than employees of Mills & Boon Limited, their agencies or anyone associated with the administration of the competition.
2. There will be six prizes of solitaire diamond rings each at an estimated retail value of £1,000 (one thousand pounds).
3. Competition closes on 21st Dec. 1983, winners will be notified by 16th Jan. 1984.
4. For results send an S.A.E. to the competition address above.

WORTH £1,000 (retail value)

ENTRY FORM:—

1. Dr Zhivago	&		A. Juliet	G. Cleopatra
2. Maria	&		B. Lara	H. Cathy
3. Rochester	&		C. Josephine	I. Jane Eyre
4. Heathcliff	&		D. Rhett Butler	
5. Antony	&		E. Emma Hamilton	
6. Nelson	&		F. Baron Von Trapp	

Tie Breaker:— Mills & Boon is the very best in romantic fiction because
(complete this sentence in not more than 12 words):

....
....

NAME (BLOCK CAPITALS PLEASE) ....
ADDRESS ....
....
BOOK PURCHASED AT ....